...go and work in the .... with his father. It was not something the family ever talked about — it was just taken for granted — and Moggy could find no good reason for going against their expectations. But he was skilful with his fists and the other boys at the North Road School had learned that they were likely to come off second best in a fight with Moggy. It was this that first gave him the idea that he might have a future as a boxer. Moggy knew that there was a very big difference between scrapping in the playground and depending for a living on his fists, but some boxers used their skill to fight their way out of dockland and Moggy was determined to do all he could to escape the poverty and insecurity of the dockie's existence.

'Set in the twenties, the book speaks to the seventies, with its strikes, its fuzz-fights, its frustrations for the urban teenager. It speaks, too, in the fights themselves, which ooze the tense sweaty ritual of the boxing ring, the whirling pain of punches, the crowd yelling blood. This is a direct and frankly dialogued story.'

The Times Educational Supplement

'It's completely engrossing; I think most boys and girls over 12 will agree with me.'

Teachers' World

DOCKIE

Martin Ballard

First published 1972 by Longman Group Limited
First published in Lions 1974
by William Collins Sons and Co Ltd
8 Grafton Street, London W1X 3LA
Second Impression September 1983

© 1972 by Martin Ballard

Printed in Great Britain
by William Collins Sons and Co Ltd, Glasgow

To Daniel

1

By long tradition, fights at North Road School always took place in the space behind the sheds at the side of the playground. It was never long before news of a punch up had spread among the pupils. Nobody wanted to miss a good spectacle, but even the youngest knew better than to run or show signs of excitement which would draw attention to the fact that something was up.

The contestants, Jan Jaworski and Moggy Harris, were an ill-matched pair. The Pole was almost a foot taller than his opponent, with well developed muscles across his upper arms and back. By far the largest boy in the school, he had been undisputed baron of his age group for as long as anyone could remember. Moggy, in contrast, was a true East-Ender: short and squat with long arms, which looked thin and pale beside those of his adversary. At fourteen he was a bare five foot tall and if the rest of the men in his family were anything to go by he had not much left to grow.

'Who started it?' asked one of the smaller onlookers.

'Harris. Gave Jaworski a right mouthful.'

The small onlooker stared at Moggy in awe. Some boys had been forced to fight the Pole but nobody went out of his way to look for trouble with him.

Jan thrust his hands out in front of him and bent low so that his eyes were almost level with the smaller boy's. Suddenly he feinted one way and then brought his left fist into his opponent's face. Moggy's head reeled and blood began to flow from his nose across his tightly drawn lips.

'Wipe your nose, titch; your chin's bleeding,' shouted a joker in the crowd.

The smile on Jan's face showed that he did not take his opponent seriously. 'Getting a big boy, are you, Mog?'

7

Jan's sneer and the taunts from the onlookers stung Moggy Harris into a blind fury. Ducking his head, he bored below his opponent's guard and landed a blow to the solar plexus. Moggy could hear the breath squeeze out of Jan's mouth. Catching the moment, he crooked his arm round the larger boy's neck, swung him round and sent him crashing to the ground. By an instinctive movement, Jaworski put his hands up to protect himself while he recovered his breath. Jan was not yet hurt, but at least he knew that he had a fight on his hands. He slowly rose to one knee and then tried to stand up, but again Moggy caught him as he struggled to regain his balance. This time, however, he managed to grab a handful of Moggy's hair as he fell, and the two boys rolled over together.

All chattering stopped as the onlookers became engrossed in the contest. The sneer had vanished from Jan's face as he concentrated on maintaining a grip on his opponent's hair. Disregarding the pain, Moggy worked himself round so that he could bring his feet into action. His boots had seen better days, but at least they were all of a piece. The Pole wore only light slippers and the sole of one was already half off.

'Cor!' The onlookers caught their breath as Moggy dug his heels into the other boy's side. In a moment of pain Jan loosed his handful of hair, and Moggy jumped to his feet. He was about to leap on to his opponent's chest when a cry from the onlookers made him freeze in his tracks, giving Jan the opportunity to regain his feet.

'Teacher, teacher!'

The master on duty had finished his tea and noticed that the whole playground was deserted. From long experience he knew where to find the trouble.

'Let me through,' shouted the teacher in a tone of voice which was rather too high-pitched to carry any menace. By now the crowd of onlookers had gone silent once again.

'You heard me. Let me through,' yelled the teacher again.

But the kids had linked arms in a solid circle to keep him away from the combatants. He made two or three ineffective attempts to break through the ring at various points before retreating to the main building once again. During the interruption the two boys circled each other, regaining their breath and looking for a way through the other's guard.

'I'll hammer you so's you won't forget, you squirt.' Jan's voice carried more of the accent of the East End than that of the Polish which he spoke at home.

Moggy looked at him as if he had not heard the taunt. When the larger boy lumbered in to the assault he used his advantage and lashed out with his boots at the other's ill-protected feet. Both Jan's fists and Moggy's boots missed their mark, but Moggy was quicker to recover his balance and he was able to barge below his opponent's guard and thrust his fists into his stomach. This time, however, Jan's muscles were tensed, ready for the blow. Once more they began to circle round each other and the onlookers relaxed enough to begin to shout encouragement again. Moggy was vaguely aware of the noise, but he neither knew nor cared whether the other kids were shouting for him or for Jan. He only knew that he must get the bigger boy on to the ground as soon as possible in order to neutralize his extra height and strength. After a couple of turns he darted forward, riding a blow to the chin as he went. His two hands lashed out blindly at any available target, while he hooked his left leg behind Jan's knees. For a moment the tall boy struggled to keep his balance. Then he fell backwards, grazing his elbow on the hard ground. Moggy was on top of him like a flash but, just as he was about to hit out, something held him back.

The crowd had gone silent, and the kids had dropped their arms. Mr Pender, the headmaster, held Moggy by the scruff of the neck and dragged him off the Pole. Then with a sharp gesture he motioned Jan to stand up. Mr Pender stood hardly more than four inches taller than Moggy and he must have been getting on for sixty, but it never crossed the mind of either boy that they might disobey him.

'What are you lot staring at?' he snapped at the on-lookers. 'Go on, all of you.'

Slowly at first, then with increasing speed, the youngsters went off to different parts of the playground, discussing the fight as they went. The two protagonists were marched by the headmaster towards the main building. Both boys had been into the head's study on a fair number of occasions, and they had never found it an agreeable experience. The little man sat down behind his desk and looked from one to the other.

'Which one of you started it?'

'He hit me first,' replied Moggy.

The head turned a cold stare on Jan, who dropped his eyes to his feet. 'We've had this before, Jaworski, haven't we? Do you enjoy fighting boys smaller than yourself?'

'Weren't me.' Jan had great difficulty in getting the words out and he shuffled his feet uneasily as he did so.

Mr Pender turned towards Moggy. 'You tell me, then. Did Jaworski start it?'

'He hit me first.'

Mr Pender looked back towards the Pole. 'Is that true? Did you hit him first?'

Jaworski looked across the study but Moggy avoided his eye. 'Yes sir,' he replied at last.

Mr Pender leant forward in his chair and banged his hand down on the desk in front of him. 'Why did you hit him?'

The violence in the headmaster's voice stung Jan to self-defence. 'Because he called me names,' he shouted. 'Nobody ain't calling me names. Not like that.'

Mr Pender's face assumed a look of long-suffering patience as he turned to Moggy. 'Did you call him names?' he asked.

'What if I did?' retorted Moggy defiantly.

Jan looked sharply sideways. The smaller boy was as

good as owning up. He only had to keep his mouth shut to leave the blame with him. Moggy knew what Jan was thinking. He would have liked to have been able to tell the Pole that he was not owning up to get him off the hook. He was not prepared to let Mr Pender go on feeling sorry for him. He wanted the headmaster to know that he was not just another kid being bullied by the baron.

Mr Pender looked from one to the other. 'I'll ask you again. Which one of you started it?'

'He called me names,' grunted Jan.

'That's no reason to hit him, is it?'

'Depends on the name, sir, don't it?'

'What did you call him?'

Moggy kept his mouth tight shut. He could not remember the actual words.

'I asked what you said.'

'Don't remember,' said Moggy under his breath.

'Do you remember enough to be able to give an opinion as to whether he was justified in hitting you?' Moggy looked at the head with a puzzled expression. 'If somebody had said something like that to you would you have hit him?'

'I ain't a bleeding Pole. I don't know what I'd do, do I?' Mr Pender sat silently, as if dissatisfied with the answer. After several seconds of silence Moggy added, 'I'd crease anyone who said it to me.'

'Then why –' Mr Pender started to press his interrogation, but then thought better of it. He walked over to the corner of his study and took out a cane. With a nod of his head he indicated to Jaworski to hold out one of his hands and gave it two swift blows. Another nod – the other hand – two more blows. A third, dismissive nod and Jan walked towards the door, his hands tucked under his armpits. The whole caning went with the smoothness of a well practised routine. Guilty or not, Jan had expected to be caned. It was the recognized sign that fighting on the school premises was not permitted.

When the door clicked shut Mr Pender returned to his

desk. Moggy looked, first one way, then the other and finally settled his gaze on the toe caps of his boots. He wanted to get the caning over, but there was obviously more talk to come first.

'How old are you, Harris?'

'Fourteen.'

'When are you leaving us?'

'End of term, sir.'

'That's only two weeks.' The head leaned back in his chair and said nothing. Moggy could feel the blood harden round his mouth, and the palms of his hands had begun to tingle. 'What are you going to do?' asked Mr Pender at last.

'Do?'

'Do for a living. Life does not end when you leave school, you know.'

'Be a dockie, I suppose. With my dad.'

'Have you thought of anything else?'

'I ain't much of a scholar, am I, sir?'

'Not a scholar, no. But there are other jobs besides working in the docks. It's very uncertain.'

'I ain't thought of nothing else.'

'Haven't thought of anything else.' Mr Pender's school-master's reactions worked instinctively.

'Sir?'

'I haven't thought of anything else is correct English.' The head looked at the boy who stood on the other side of his desk as if he wanted to reach him in some way, but Moggy had drawn himself up and looked fixedly at the wall. He realized that, having dealt with Jan Jaworski in the first moment of outraged authority, Mr Pender no longer wanted to beat him. The moment passed, the caning would have to be cold-blooded.

'You might find a job as a carpenter.' The discussion on his future gave a last flicker. Moggy did not answer, nor was an answer expected of him.

Moggy was not so practised in the routine of caning as

Jan had been, so Mr Pender had to translate his instructions into words.

'Left hand.'

'Right hand.'

Three on each – hard enough – satisfied the demands of justice. Unconsciously copying Jan, Moggy tucked his hands under his armpits as he walked towards the door. But Mr Pender did not let him go in peace.

'Harris. You've only got two weeks. Keep out of trouble. I don't want to have to cane you again before you leave us.'

'I won't fight in school, sir.'

'Try not to fight anywhere.'

'Can I go now, sir?'

'Yes. Rejoin your class. School has started. You'd better wash first.'

'Thank you, sir.'

As he closed the door, Moggy wondered why he had thanked Mr Pender. For beating him? For making a few half-baked remarks about what he was going to do when he left school? He studied the marks across his hands as he walked down the dim corridor towards the washroom. Everyone seemed to end up by thanking Mr Pender. Even dockers who had left North Road School nearly twenty years before spoke as if they had got something to thank him for. Moggy decided that he had got nothing to thank Mr Pender for – or to thank any teacher for, when it came to that.

Moggy's classmates were quick to assure him that Jaworski would be waiting for him outside school. It was normal practice that, when fights were interrupted inside school premises, they should be finished outside. Sitting at his desk, Moggy would have been glad enough for the whole stupid business to be forgotten. His nose was still tender, and the weals made by the cane stood out on the palms of his hands. He recognized, however, that Jan had more to lose by calling it quits than he had. At the moment that Mr Pender had broken up the fight Moggy had held the upper hand. And, as the bigger boy, Jan was expected to win.

When the bell finally went, Moggy was in no hurry to move. His young brother Charlie found him in the corridor when most of the others had already gone. Charlie was about an inch taller than his older brother, but his body had not yet filled out.

'Why did you fight the Pole, Mog?' asked Charlie in an awed voice. 'The kids say you started it.'

Moggy was not at all sure just why he had started it. He could only recall the argument before the fight in the vaguest way. As far as he could remember, he had called Jan 'Polski'. Jan had retorted, in a good humoured-enough tone of voice, with some comment like, 'Watch it, titch.' For years Moggy had put up with being called titch, nipper, half pint, short arse and many other names. But that particular day the reference to his size got him on the raw. From what he could remember he had started calling Jan all sorts of names. He had surprised himself and all the onlookers with his eloquence. Since Jan was no match for Moggy in a slanging match, he really had had no option but to aim a knuckle sandwich at his face.

'My mates reckon you beat him.' Charlie laughed. 'Cor! You should have seen his phiz when you hit him in the gut.'

'Knocked his bloody smile off, didn't I?'

Acting out the scene, Charlie grasped his stomach and screwed up his face. 'Blimey,' he added. 'And when you dug your boots into his side. Bet he's got a hell of a bruise there.'

Moggy fingered the end of his nose. 'Caught me all right, though.'

'How's your conk? Does it hurt?'

'Course it bleeding well hurts, half wit.'

'Going to finish him off, Mog?'

Charlie's easy enthusiasm suddenly grated on Moggy.

'It's better than evens he'll finish me, ain't it?'

Charlie missed the anxiety in his brother's voice. 'Don't be soft, Mog. You had him beat. He's –'

'Shut up, can't you?'

Turning away, Moggy walked off, along the corridor and down the stairs. After pausing for a moment, Charlie followed a yard or so behind.

Although Moggy was one of the last out of the building, very few of the pupils had set off for home. The short alley between the school gates and Cable Street was lined with children of all ages. A cold March wind was blowing up from the river, funnelling between the tall tenement buildings which flanked the alley, and a number of the youngsters stamped and slapped their arms around their bodies to keep warm. The more fortunate were protected by an odd variety of top clothing. Some of the older boys wore working men's jackets, which had seen service at the dock side. Others wore blazers and jackets which mothers and aunts had picked up when charring in the better class suburbs, or which had found their way on to the second-hand clothing stalls in the street markets. Some of the girls had nothing more than a light dress to keep out the wind.

As he walked through the school gate into the alley, with Charlie close on his heels, Moggy was only conscious of a sea of faces. He could even see women peering through the washing strung across the balconies of the tenements. Jaworski was standing in a doorway, surrounded by a number of his friends.

'Do you want to finish the fight?' asked Moggy.

'Ah, have a go at someone your own bleeding size,' snapped Jan.

At lunch-time the insult would have made Moggy fighting mad, but now the anger had gone out of him. 'Scared, are you?' he retorted.

'Look, Harris,' said the Pole through clenched teeth, 'I could do for you. If you really want to fight I could beat the living daylights out of you.'

'Show him, Mog,' urged Charlie.

Moggy had to tilt his head backwards to look Jan in the eye. The bigger boy was giving him the option of whether or not to fight, and Moggy could hardly kid himself that it was because he was scared.

'It weren't so easy before. What makes you think you could do for me now, Polski?'

'I'll show you, if you want to find out.'

Looking for action rather than talk, the onlookers began to press in around them.

'Ain't you going to finish him off, Mog?'

With a swift movement Jan dragged a skinny lad from the front rank of the crowd. 'Was that you shouted?' he asked. The boy's body shook helplessly as he nodded. Jan looked him up and down. 'You're taller than Moggy. Tell you what, I'll take you on instead.' He called out to the crowd. 'That all right?'

Most of the onlookers realized that the fight they had been waiting for was not going to take place, so they adjusted themselves to get what amusement they could at the expense of the boy who had spoken out of turn.

'Here, hold his coat,' said Jaworski to one of his friends. The boy clutched his jacket tight around himself as Jan tried to peel it off his back. Then he had to duck out of range as the big Pole tormented him with the palms of his hands. Tears were streaming down his cheeks when Jan finally grabbed him by the collar.

'Look, squirt,' he said. 'If Moggy and I have something to fight about we'll do it our own way. We ain't fighting so's you can have an eye-full.' He looked around him and shouted, 'That goes for the lot of you.'

Moggy had been prepared to fight it out – even if he was going to get beaten – but he was glad enough not to have to. The two of them pushed their way through the crowd and walked into Cable Street.

'Don't call me names,' said Jan when they were out of earshot of the others. Moggy's silence implied agreement. 'I could hammer you, like I said,' he added. 'But, for your size, you're bloody good; I'll give you that.' He turned towards the railway arches on the north side of the street.

'See you, then,' said Moggy.

Jan nodded and walked off on his own. Moggy stuck his hands in his pockets as he strolled down Cable Street. Charlie ran a few steps to catch up with him.

'He was afraid to go on,' jeered Charlie.

Moggy laughed. 'Don't be bloody stupid.'

'You should have made him, Mog.'

'Look, kid. I ain't getting myself clobbered just to give you a big thrill. If you're that keen you can fight him yourself.'

'You know, you ought to take up boxing,' said Charlie seriously.

'Oh, chuck it,' snapped Moggy.

Charlie tried to reopen the conversation twice on the way along Cable Street, but Moggy would not talk any more about the fight against the Pole or about fighting in general. There did not seem much else to talk about, so they walked home in silence.

The Harris family had a house to themselves with their own front door – which was more than could be said of a large proportion of the families which sent children to North Road School. Number 6 Albert Street was in the middle of a row of little terraced houses. It had two bedrooms upstairs and a living-room and scullery downstairs. At the back there was a little yard, at the bottom of which was a lavatory. Ever since the Water Board had put mains down the street at the end of the nineteenth century, the residents had looked forward to the day when the landlord would install water closets. Now in the early twenties there was still no sign of him getting round to it, so they had to make do with old-fashioned thunder boxes.

Moggy always felt that the house was too full of people. He was the second of six children. His older sister had left home the year before to become a 'slavey' in a house in North London, and she got so little holiday that they hardly ever saw her. But, as if to make up for her departure, number seven was on the way. In bad times his parents even took in the odd lodger, who had to fit in as best he could. Mercifully there was no lodger in residence at the moment, but Mrs Harris in her pregnant condition almost counted for two.

Mrs Harris looked on the house as her territory from the time that her husband left for work in the morning until the children came in from school in the afternoon. Doris and the baby, who were too young to go to school, got under-foot from time to time, but at least they did not challenge her authority. She always declared that the worst thing for a docker's wife was the fact that you could never be certain, once your husband had gone out in the morning, that you had seen the back of him for the day. When Curly Harris failed to find work or got himself laid off early he was in trouble on two counts. In the first place, he was not providing the money expected of him; in the second place his carcass was sure to be planted in the wrong place at the wrong time.

When Moggy and Charlie came in through the front door they found their father sitting with a friend, arranging dominoes on the table. Each man had a small pile of coppers at his elbow. Moggy only nodded in their direction as he crossed the room and sat down in a chair.

'No work, Dad?' asked Charlie.

Moggy clenched his fists. His brother never knew when to keep his mouth buttoned. Mrs Harris emerged from the scullery and walked across behind her husband.

'He got four hours this morning, that's all. Now he's giving his money away. Don't blame me if there ain't no supper.'

Moggy braced himself, ready for an argument, but on this occasion his father decided to play deaf. For several minutes the room was silent except for the click of dominoes and the scraping of coins across the table. Mrs Harris moved backwards and forwards, ostensibly on household tasks, watching out of the corner of her eye to see which way the money was going. On one of her journeys she noticed Moggy's face and clothes.

'What have you been doing to yourself, may I ask?'

'He had a fight,' volunteered Charlie.

Mr Harris took his eyes off the dominoes for a moment and looked round at his eldest son.

'He beat a great strapper,' added Charlie. 'The biggest boy in the school.'

Mrs Harris hauled Moggy to his feet and checked over his clothes. 'If you've torn these bags – '

'They ain't torn,' retorted Moggy irritably. 'Nothing's torn.'

'What about your face, then?'

'That'll mend,' snapped her husband. He turned to Moggy. 'What about the other geezer?'

'You should just see him,' boasted Moggy. In his own mind he was already beginning to exaggerate the injuries he had inflicted on the big Pole.

Mr Harris turned back to the table and pushed a domino on to the end of the row. 'Not bad for a nipper?' he grunted to his friend. 'He's tough for a half pint.'

After a few more moves the game finished. Curly Harris picked up all the coppers and counted them out into two piles. 'Here you are, woman.' He shoved one pile of coins to the edge of the table. 'That'll buy an inside lining for this lot.'

'Oh, you won for once, did you?' his wife said sarcastically, swiftly sweeping the coins into her hand. 'We're allowed to eat, are we?' As Mr Harris and his friend got up from the table and walked towards the door she added, 'We could eat better still with the other half.'

'You make do with what I've given you.'

'What if you don't get work tomorrow?'

'Look, woman, them's my wages. I'll do what I like with my money.'

'Spend it in the boozer.'

'Mind your own business.'

Mr Harris ushered his friend out and slammed the door

after him. His wife gathered herself and then looked down to count the coins in her hand. 'Here!' She held out a shilling towards Charlie. 'Run off to the market.'

Charlie took the money reluctantly. 'What do you want?'

'A bit of mutton. Oh yes – get some vegetables too: potatoes and a swede.'

Charlie looked down at the coin in his hand. 'All for a shilling?'

'That should be plenty. Eightpence for the meat –'

'Things ain't as cheap as they was,' interrupted Charlie. 'You'd know that if you ever went to market yourself.'

'Don't be cheeky.'

Reluctantly Mrs Harris took another threepence and handed them over to Charlie. Moggy reckoned that his young brother had negotiated at least a penny or twopence for sweets for himself on the side. The great thing about the market was that prices were never the same from one stall to the next so it was impossible for anybody to check on how much had been spent. Swiftly Charlie pocketed the money and disappeared before his mother could think again.

'When's supper?' asked Moggy.

'When it's cooked,' she replied sharply. 'I ain't even got the meat yet, have I?'

'It'll be hours,' complained Moggy. 'I'm hungry.'

His mother could not resist taking advantage of the opening offered her. 'If you didn't waste your energies fighting, you wouldn't get so hungry, would you?'

'Got some bread and jam?'

'Here!' She took a penny from her hand and held it out to him. 'You can get a bun with that.'

'Thanks.' Moggy knew that he was getting money rather than a slice off the loaf because it took him out of the house. He looked forward to the time when he would earn his own money so that he would not have to beg coppers off his parents.

'While you're out you can go and look for the girls.'

'Where are they?'

'If I knew I wouldn't send you to look, would I?'

'What do you want me to tell them?'

'Just see what they're up to. That Bet should have been at school today. Did you see her?'

'No. Then I wouldn't. She's always with her own friends.'

Bet had such a hatred of being shut up in a class-room all day that Mrs Harris had a job to know when she was at school and when she was not. She went out at the proper time every morning, but all too often she never got as far as North Road; she joined up instead with a pack of friends who spent their time roaming the streets. On the days when she did go to school, she rushed off to meet up with the gang the moment they let her out. In recent months the School Board Officer had been clamping down on her, and the message had just begun to dawn on her that she would have to be educated, whether she liked it or not. Doris, at five, was not old enough to go to school. Although young for Bet's gang, she attached herself to it and fiercely resisted any attempts to shake her off.

Once he had armed himself with a large penny bun, Moggy set off at a leisurely pace to search the streets for his sisters. He ran them to earth surprisingly easily in a courtyard, not a hundred yards from the house. Bet was skipping with another girl of her own age on a single rope, while the others stood around in a circle, chanting the rhythm.

> 'Sam, Sam, you dirty old man,
>   Washed your face in the frying pan,
>   Combed your hair
>   With the leg of a chair,
>   Sam, Sam, you dirty old man.'

As soon as she saw him, Doris disengaged herself from the circle and ran across to Moggy. She tore off a piece of the half bun which he still held in his hand and shoved it into her mouth.

Bet and her friend were doing well and the children started to chant a second time, but the rope became tangled in their legs, before they had finished the first line.

'Hallo, Moggy,' shouted Bet. 'You had a fight?'

'How do you know?' asked Moggy.

'I was there, weren't I? I saw you.'

'Went to school, did you?'

' 'Course I went to school,' replied Bet, outraged. She walked across, trailing the skipping rope behind her to examine her brother for damage. Embarrassed, Moggy spun her round and pulled the rope from her hand.

'See you skip,' shouted one of Bet's friends.

'Come on, Mog,' urged Bet. 'Show us how.'

Moggy looked at the rope. 'I ain't a girl.'

'Ain't only girls that skip,' protested one of the gang, who Moggy only knew as Liz. 'What about the puggies?' She took the rope from his hand and began to skip – first one foot, then the other – in the lazy way used by boxers in training.

'Where did you learn that?' asked Moggy.

'My uncle was a boxer,' replied Liz. 'He showed me.'

'Here, let me have a go.'

Before he tried to skip, Moggy checked round the courtyard to make sure that nobody was watching. At first the rope got tangled round his feet, but, after several attempts, he managed to get the rhythm. His movements were clumsier than the girl's had been, but he soon got into the swing of it.

'I'll skip with you,' called Bet when the rope finally tangled in his feet. She ran over and stood facing him, almost touching. 'You hold the rope.'

Moggy pushed her away and shook his head. 'Supper's going to be late,' he said.

'How late?' asked Bet.

'Two hours at least,' guessed Moggy. 'I'm off.'

'Where are you going?' asked Bet.

22

Moggy shrugged his shoulders. After a moment's hesitation Bet decided to tag along behind him. The others followed, leaving Doris trying to skip with the rope which had been abandoned in the middle of the courtyard.

'I saw the fight,' repeated Bet.

'So you told me.'

'Big weren't he.'

'The bigger they are the harder they fall,' chanted one of her friends. 'He didn't half go a wallop.'

Bet caught hold of his arm. 'You was great, Mog. Going to be a puggy when you leave school?'

'Who gave you that idea?'

'All the kids say you should.'

The girl called Liz ran round in front of them and peered up at Moggy's face. 'Here, you got a proper noser, didn't you?' She lunged out to grab his nose, but Moggy pulled his head away in time. 'Does it hurt?' she asked.

'It will if you bash it.'

'You should see my uncle's snout,' said Liz. 'It's all big and spread out.'

'Runs in the family, don't it?' jeered Bet. She turned to the rest of the gang. 'Ain't she got the ugliest snitch you've ever seen?'

'I ain't.' Liz turned her face towards Moggy for an impartial judgement.

Moggy examined it from all angles. 'It's a very beautiful nose,' he pronounced.

'There you are!' declared Liz triumphantly.

'Him!' retorted Bet. 'He can't see straight. Blinded by love.'

The other girls shrieked with laughter and tried to push Liz towards Moggy. She fought her way out of their grasp, and then had the quickness of wit to divert their attention from their joke.

'Look, there's Lushy Sue,' she shouted.

A hunched figure in long black rags was hobbling along the other side of the road, her cracked boots splashing in the gutter. The gang crossed the road, formed itself up behind her and followed at a safe distance. Bet set the rhythm as they chanted the ditty they had made up specially for her benefit.

> 'Lushy Sue, Lushy Sue,
> Look what gin has done to you.
> Since you washed is very long,
> Oh by crikey, don't you pong.'

'She's a witch,' hissed Liz at Moggy.

' 'Course she ain't a witch,' contradicted Bet. 'Got alcohol instead of blood, that's all.' She turned to Moggy and spoke in an oddly precise voice. 'Mum says that Lushy Sue's unhappy because she was crossed in love.'

'Could happen to you,' teased Moggy. 'I can just see you in sixty years' time.' He shuffled along the gutter in a passable imitation of the old woman. 'Lushy Bet they'll call you. And all the time you'll be pining away for lost love.'

'No,' announced Bet. 'I'm going to marry a swell. I'll visit you sometimes and slip you a tanner or two before I go back to my big house.'

Moggy looked at his sister and laughed. She was barefoot and her dress had been washed to a faded grey. Her face and hands carried the grime of days on the streets. Still, he thought, she could grow up to be a trim enough little doll.

'You'd better say hallo to some soap and water before you go looking for a swell,' he remarked.

But Bet was not to be deflected from her day-dream. 'Perhaps I won't give you no money after all.'

'Stingy thing.'

'I won't have to. You'll be a world champion, and you'll have piles of oof of your own by then.'

'Some hopes of that,' grunted Moggy.

'You don't know, do you?' mused Bet.

'As much chance as there is of you marrying a swell, I suppose.'

'My beauty and your muscle.' Bet tried to catch a glimpse of herself in a window. 'Ain't I beautiful?'

She did not notice that the others had stopped till she bumped into one of them. Lushy Sue had turned to face her tormentors. She looked from one to the other and then filled her lungs.

'Piss off,' she shouted. 'Piss off, I tell you.'

Bet braced her body and stepped defiantly forward. Holding her breath she stared into the old woman's bloodshot eyes. For fully thirty seconds they glared at each other, while the gang watched, fascinated. At last Lushy Sue's eyes hooded and her jaws snapped open and shut. The sudden movement was too much for Bet. The pent up breath exploded from her mouth as she turned on her heels and ran off, followed closely by the others.

It was only by a firm exercise in self-control that Moggy saved himself from the indignity of flight. Assuming as casual an air as he could muster he strolled towards Lushy Sue, catching her powerful aroma of mingled dirt and gin as he did so. She turned warily to watch him pass, and then spat on to the pavement behind him.

Moggy looked back at the saliva on the pavement. 'Dirty beast,' he sneered.

'Bugger off,' yelled Lushy Sue in a shrill voice.

Moggy's new found talent for abuse seemed to have deserted him. 'Don't use naughty words,' he retorted lamely.

The old woman said nothing, but glared suspiciously at her enemy as he walked on with as casual a stride as he could manage.

Moggy was soon able to put Lushy Sue out of his mind. The day had given him other, more pressing things to think about. He could still feel the weals made by Mr Pender's stick across the palms of his hands and his nose was tender to the touch. But these physical mementoes of the day's events were unimportant.

By bringing up the question of what he was going to do when he left school Mr Pender had given him food for

25

thought. Until that moment Moggy had never actually enjoyed being at North Road School, but it had seemed the inevitable – the only – place to be. Now he realized for the first time that he was on the point of leaving.

Deep in his mind he knew that he had to distinguish reality from day-dreams. The reality was that he would have to start earning as soon as term was finished. Of course the headmaster was right when he warned him of the hardships of a docker's life. But Moggy knew that, as a dockie's son, he had a start over the casual labourers. With a bit of luck before long he would get a ticket like his dad and have first chance of whatever work was going.

But, after the drama of the afternoon, Moggy could not resist a bit of day-dreaming. Being so much smaller than Jaworski it did not really matter to him that the fight had been left unfinished. All the kids were talking about him becoming a puggy. Both Charlie and Bet had said so. Moggy knew that there was a big difference between scrapping in the playground and depending on his fists for a living. As a boxer life would have an uncertainty which both frightened and fascinated him. At worst he could end up with nothing but a disfigured face to show for his pains. But some boxers became champions. They used their fists to fight their way out of dockland.

Moggy reminded himself that it was only a day-dream. But nobody could stop him living a bit on day-dreams if he wanted to.

2

During the last two weeks of school nothing seemed permanent any more. The regimentation of school life, which Moggy had always before taken for granted, now got on his nerves. Every morning the boys paraded in the playground to do Swedish drill under the eagle eye of the teachers. Before the exercises started they were lined up in precise rows, dressed off from the front, with just three feet between each boy. Then they went through the movements in perfect co-ordination. Mr Pender always took a pride in the standard of drill at his school, and those who broke the rhythm were rapidly singled out for punishment. Moggy had never before had any difficulty in keeping time with the others, but twice during the last two weeks the master in charge had jumped into the ranks and cuffed his ear to encourage his concentration. It was not that Moggy was consciously trying to break things up; his old, ingrained reactions were just not working properly.

He found life easier in the classroom. The teachers had long since learned not to expect too much in the way of work out of him and, as long as he kept his mouth shut when he was supposed to, they were happy enough to let him think his own thoughts.

Mr Pender had really set Moggy's mind going. The headmaster had suggested carpentry as a possible trade, but had not offered any suggestion about how Moggy could set about finding an apprenticeship. Occasionally he saw notices announcing that some craftsman or other was looking for a boy, but Moggy had an idea that they would not think much of taking on a docker's son.

Everyone at home assumed that, when he finished school, he would go to the docks with his dad. It was not something they talked about; it was just taken for granted. And Moggy could not find any good reason for going against what was expected of him.

The school windows were set high in the walls to prevent pupils from staring out when they should have been paying attention to lessons. From his desk Moggy could only see the tops of the warehouses that lined the north side of the river. Above their roofs the cranes of the Surrey Docks made angular patterns against the sky. When the teacher's back was turned he sometimes stood for a moment to see whether he could catch a glimpse of any traffic on the river through the narrow gaps between the warehouses. Even when he could not see the ships he could hear the noise of their hooters – the high-pitched note of the tug-boats and the deep call of the ocean-going vessels. As he listened Moggy projected himself into a dockie's life. His father stored up information in his brain on all the movement of shipping on the river. He knew which vessels carried dirty cargoes, to be avoided except in extremity; which carried perishables, needing to be unloaded without delay. Most important, he knew which docks were likely to be busy and which idle.

When Moggy was not thinking about the docks he was day-dreaming about boxing. Charlie and Bet had started something going in his mind. Being small was a disadvantage when it came to taking on someone the size of Jaworski, but, in the fight game, size did not count for much. In a properly organized ring he would only fight opponents his own size.

During the remaining two weeks of school Moggy had further opportunities to test his strength against other pupils. He did not go round looking for fights, but several boys had the idea of pitting themselves against the lad who had got one over the big Pole. In all Moggy had to fight three more times behind the shed, and each time he won without too much trouble. Before the end of term the other boys were treating him with respect. On the evidence available, Moggy had as much chance of making a go of it in the ring as any of them. But he knew that he would not achieve anything in a hurry and, in the mean-time, he had to earn a living like everybody else.

On the last day of term he stood in a line of boys and girls who were leaving school and listened while Mr Pender spoke to them for the last time. They were going out into the world where they would be faced with great challenges and grave temptations. Their task was to make the best of the challenges which life offered and to resist the temptations. Mr Pender hoped that they would all return the benefits which society had given them, in the shape of their education at North Road School, by giving an honest day's work for a good day's wages.

Moggy stared at Mr Pender as he spoke. The man had taught dockers' children for twenty years and presumably he knew how things were. The kids he was speaking to would be lucky indeed to do two honest days' work a week, whether they wanted to or not. As for a good day's wages – that depended on how you looked at it.

They ended up by singing a hymn:

'O God our help in ages past,
Our hope for years to come,
Our shelter from the stormy blast,
And our eternal home.'

As always on the last day of term the kids sang loudly, and without any sense of the words. A couple of the boys who were leaving did their best to lag a few beats behind the piano but as soon as Mr Pender singled them out with his eye they fell into time with the rest. Moggy wondered how long it would be before he sang another hymn. With a bit of luck, he thought, he could get by until one of the family got married. Perhaps it would be in a big West End church when Bet was getting spliced to her swell. Moggy stopped singing and grinned behind the hymn book at the thought. When he looked up he discovered that Mr

Pender's eye had lighted on him. He began to sing with the rest:

> 'Before the shadow of thy throne,
> Thy saints have dwelt secure . . .'

but he kept thinking of Bet. If anyone could wangle herself a big house with lots of slaveys to look after her, that one might. Stranger things had happened.

When the service was over Mr Pender stood at the door and said goodbye to the leavers one by one.

'I'm sorry you found the service funny, Harris,' he said.

'It weren't the service, sir,' Moggy stammered.

'Thinking your own thoughts, were you? Don't do that when you're on the docks or you'll find yourself under a crate.'

'No, sir.'

Mr Pender held out his hand and Moggy took it clumsily. 'Come back and see us, won't you?'

'Yes, sir,' replied Moggy. He knew that he would not. Enough was enough.

He walked out of the iron gate and up the alley next to Jan Jaworski, who was also leaving. They had not spoken since the day of the fight.

'How are you going to crack a crust, Polski?' asked Moggy.

'Reckon I'll join the army.'

'No, I mean straight up.'

'I ain't kidding,' Jan assured him. 'They'll take me when I'm fifteen. I'll just mooch about till then.'

'But it's the bleeding British army,' protested Moggy.

'I was born here, weren't I?'

'Suit yourself,' said Moggy. 'I wouldn't join up and have some Hun shove his bayonet in my breadbasket.'

'The next war won't be against the Germans,' replied Jan.

'How do you know anything about the next war?'

'My dad gets about. He's a sailor.'

30

'Who does he reckon you'll be fighting, then?' asked Moggy.

'Britain and Germany will be allies against the commies.'

Moggy thought about the idea. 'I can't see a Russian bayonet would be that different from a German – once it was stuck in.'

Jan changed the subject. 'What're you going to do?'

Moggy shrugged. 'Docks, I suppose.'

'Just because your dad's a dockie don't mean you've got to be one too.'

'It's as good as the army,' retorted Moggy.

'I wouldn't be seen dead as a dockie.'

'They're choosy who they take on.'

'Christ!' exclaimed Jan. 'You'd think they were doing you a favour, giving you a card.'

'There's worse jobs.'

Jan shrugged. 'Suppose it's all right so long as you don't mind starving to death every now and then.'

'At least they don't order you about, like in the bleeding army.'

'Here, what's your dad been telling you? You'll find a right load of bastards down there.' He turned and looked at Moggy. 'Ain't you got no ambition?'

Moggy had an ambition, but preferred not to talk about it. 'We'll see who's better off,' he replied sharply.

'Will I see you?' asked Jan.

Moggy was surprised. The Pole had never bothered with him until they had their fight. 'I'll be around,' he replied.

'I'll keep an eye open for you, dockie.'

Space for sleeping was distinctly limited in the Harris household. The main bedroom upstairs was almost filled up by a huge double bed which was occupied by the parents. For more than sixteen years there had always been a tenant for the cot which stood on Mrs Harris's side of the bed. The baby – now eighteen months old – could be expected to keep his place in it for another two to three months. When number seven arrived Bet and Doris would be expected to move over to make room for him in their bed which was in a tiny room with a sloping roof above the scullery.

Moggy and Charlie had in their time occupied the cot, and then the other bed upstairs. Now they slept on mattresses in the main living-room. Moggy always envied the fact that the others were free to go to sleep when they liked. There was nothing to stop the girls going up to their own room and Charlie had the marvellous ability to go over in any place at any time. It did not matter what sort of noise was going on around him; if Charlie was tired, he would just drag out his mattress and go to sleep.

Moggy could never even try to settle until the house was quiet. Even then, if his father was still out, he would generally lie awake until he came in. Moggy would always watch him through slit eyes as he came through the front door and picked his way across the room. On the nights when he seemed drunk Moggy would close his eyes again, and pretend to be asleep. At other times he would sit up on his mattress and call his father over to him. Mr Harris never found it easy to talk to any of his children, but it was easiest in the darkness, when everyone else was asleep.

This particular night Moggy lay awake for at least two hours after the rest of the house was quiet. Then, some time after midnight, the door opened and he saw his father's stocky figure outlined against the pale gaslight of the alley.

'Dad,' called Moggy. He wanted to talk that night, whether his father was drunk or not.

'Not asleep yet?'

'No. Been to the boozer?'

'We worked late.'

'Not this late.'

'Half past nine. Overtime's good money, kid.'

'It must have been dark.'

'You'll learn to work in the dark.' Mr Harris gave his

son a playful cuff. 'Reckon I deserved to heat my flues a bit, don't you?' For a time he stood awkwardly over his son. 'Left school?' he asked at last.

'That's right. Mr Pender shook us by the hand and told us to do an honest day's work for a fair day's pay.'

'Fat lot he knows about it. Mind you,' added Mr Harris thoughtfully, 'I'm not sure I'd like to be a teacher myself.'

'I've had enough of teachers, I can tell you.'

'Do you want a bit of a holiday?'

'Not much point, is there?'

Mr Harris sat down on his son's mattress. 'Funny,' he mused.

'What's funny?'

'Don't seem so long ago you were only knee high to a gnat.'

'I ain't so ruddy big now, am I?'

'No, but you're a tough little geezer. Tough enough to be a dockie.' He grabbed his son round the shoulders and wrestled him back on to the bed. 'You can't beat your dad yet, though.'

'I'll have to get into training.'

'You'll get all the training you need at work.' He paused for a moment, and then asked, 'Coming with me in the morning, Moggy?'

'There don't seem no point in waiting.' Moggy noticed that at no time had either of his parents asked him whether he was happy about being a docker.

'You couldn't pick a better time to start, kid. There's hardly a berth empty. It's the wool ships that does it. The wool ships from Australia. They take some bloody handling.'

'Are we going to the wool sales, then?'

'Not on your life. They'll all be there. Casuals and all. Let them do the hard stuff. I reckon it'll be all right up at the East India. There won't be nobody left on the stones tomorrow, I'll tell you that. Here.'

In the darkness Moggy had not noticed that his father had been carrying a paper parcel. He dropped it on the mattress, and then hauled himself to his feet and lit the lamp in the corner of the room.

'Is it for me?' asked Moggy.

'Don't get excited, kid. It ain't much of a present.'

Inside the packet was a coarse jacket with a leather shoulder and a working man's cap.

Moggy smiled. 'I've got the clobber and all.'

'If you're going to be a dockie, we've got to have you looking like one.' He looked hard into his son's face, and then he remembered something. 'Has your mum got any scissors?'

'I think there's some in the table drawer.'

Mr Harris went over to the table which stood beside the stove and rummaged about until he came out with a pair of scissors. Then he sat down on Moggy's mattress. Putting his hand to his son's head he pulled his hair over his eyes. 'You'd better have it cut a bit.'

Though far from drunk, Mr Harris had a good load of beer on board and his hand was not completely steady as he snipped his son's hair into a fringe and then trimmed it round the back into the style which set dock workers apart from other mortals. He looked at his handiwork uncertainly. 'It'll get by. Your mother can tidy it up for you tomorrow.' Mr Harris clumsily ruffled his son's hair in a gesture of affection. 'We'll make a grand docker of you, son.' He turned down the light and groped his way across the room.

'Time to doss down,' he announced. 'Don't lie awake thinking about the morning. I'll boot you out of bed in time.'

Moggy listened to his father as he stumbled up to bed. Then, in the darkness, he tried on the cap his father had bought him. It was not new, and he could smell the sweat from its previous owner's head. It was also a shade on the small side. He thought of trying on the coat but decided against it. Suddenly he felt tired. He turned over a few times to make himself comfortable on the hard mattress and then sank into sleep.

He woke next morning before it was fully light. As soon as he heard a movement upstairs, he jumped off his mattress and slipped into his working clothes. His mother was first down.

'Crikey!' she exclaimed when she saw him standing in the middle of the floor ready to go out. 'Your dad's fitted you up ready, has he? Let's see your gor blimey.'

Moggy put his cap on his head and stood to be inspected. 'It's a bit small,' he commented.

His mother pulled the cap sharply over his ears. 'You won't get another till you can buy it yourself.' For a moment she looked at him thoughtfully. 'I suppose you're as well off at the docks as anywhere,' she said brusquely. 'There ain't no easy money for the likes of us.'

She cut a doorstep off the loaf and pushed it across the table with a hunk of cheese. 'Get yourself round this. It'll help keep the draughts out.'

Moggy chewed at the bread and cheese while his mother prepared two piles of bread and cold meat and then wrapped them up in large handkerchiefs. 'I suppose you can eat as much as your dad,' she grunted. 'It's a long day if the work's there.'

'Dad says the ships are in.'

'Hope to God he's right. I don't want two of you kicking your heels round the house all day. One's bad enough.'

Upstairs the baby began to cry.

'Can't that bloody creature ever shut up?' she complained.

'I should have thought you'd enough kids to get on with,' put in Moggy.

Mrs Harris looked down at her protruding stomach. 'Blame your dad for that.' She gave the knots in the two handkerchiefs a final tug and then turned to go upstairs. 'I won't tell you to enjoy yourself,' she said. 'Just bring the money home.'

'That's a fine way to send your son off to work,' said Mr Harris as he passed her on the stairs.

'What do you think I'm going to do all day?' She

35

trudged upstairs, and shortly afterwards the sound of the baby crying ceased. In the corner of the room Charlie stirred, as if disturbed by the silence. He sat up briefly, looked over at Moggy, and then lay down and went to sleep again.

Mr Harris's eyes were bleary from the previous night's drinking and his chin carried a day's growth. 'I ain't got time to shave,' he announced. 'Not if we're going to make the East India dock in good time.'

'Do we have to go so far?'

'Just leave it to me, will you? You'll learn soon.'

'Mum gave me some bread and cheese,' said Moggy. 'Do you want any?'

His father screwed up his face in disgust. 'I couldn't eat. Come on.' He picked up his handkerchief, threw Moggy his, and led the way out into the street.

Moggy had not often been out and about so early in the morning. Quite a few adults were hurrying to work but everything was unnaturally peaceful. In an hour or two the street would fill with youngsters. Even in term time there were always kids about : little ones like Doris; kids who were officially sick, and kids who were just playing truant. In holiday time the streets seethed with children. Adults grumbled and longed for the school to start again. Hard pressed mums complained that teachers got more holiday than was good for them. But at six in the morning – in holiday as well as term time – the streets were reserved for adults. For the first time Moggy fully realized that he had moved into a new sphere of existence.

'Morning, Curly,' shouted a man from the other side of the road.

'Morning, Fred,' replied Mr Harris.

'Where's it today, then?'

'We're going to the East India. Reckon there'll be work there with all the casuals at the wool sales.'

'You might be right at that.' Fred came over and joined up with them. 'Who's the nipper, then?'

36

'My son, Moggy,' replied Mr Harris.

'I haven't seen him with you before.'

'Just starting today.'

'Another recruit for the union?' asked Fred.

'He's got enough to do without getting involved with no union,' said Mr Harris sharply.

'And he'd be a lot worse off without it too,' retorted his friend. 'He's a lot to learn.'

'He don't want to hear it now,' put in Mr Harris. 'Not at this time in the morning.'

'He's got to hear it sometime. Fat lot he'd ever get from you.'

'Christ, Fred. Do you dream about the union?' demanded Curly Harris. 'Give us a break – it's too early.'

'It's always either too early or too late for you, mate. Like it's too bleeding early or too bleeding late to pay your subscription.'

Mr Harris turned to Moggy. 'You'll meet geezers like Fred on the docks. Got one idea and never give it a rest.'

'I haven't noticed that you've got so many ideas yourself, Curly.'

'Ah, but I know what's important, don't I? Live for the union and it's all in the future. At least I can get my maulers round a pint of bitter.'

'That's the philosophy of the lumpen proletariat. You'd die a happy slave, Curly, so long as you could wet your whistle every night. You're the kind of worker the bosses pray for.'

Mr Harris nudged Moggy. 'They all go on like this. Don't do no one any harm as long as you don't take them seriously. But I say, stuff a bloke who tried to reform you at six in the morning.'

'I'm not trying to reform you, Curly. Gave that up years ago. Just dropping a word in the boy's ear before he reaches the dock gates.'

'Sowing the seed. You're just like a preacher.' He turned to Moggy. 'If the union can get you another two pence an hour then take it and be thankful. It's all good boozing money. But don't get taken in by all this guff about the great world these geezers are going to build. It's all my eye and Betty Martin.'

'Here endeth the gospel according to Curly Harris,' put in Fred Keegan.

'He'll see if I ain't right,' replied Mr Harris.

The argument over, they trudged on in silence, through Wapping and Poplar. The houses in the East India Dock Road were coming to life as maids, many of whom were little more than children, pulled back the curtains, arranged the lace drapes in front of the aspidistras and lit the fires in readiness for the respectable shopkeepers and their families to come downstairs. Trams rattled along the centre of the street, taking the early workers westwards towards town. The movement from west to east mainly consisted of dockers, hurrying to get themselves good positions for the morning call. Friends shouted to one another across the street, passing information about where the ships, which had come in on the night tide, had berthed and how many men were likely to be needed at each dock. As they approached the gate the crowd grew thicker until at last Moggy found himself wedged tight in a mass of jostling men.

'We've got a quarter of an hour to wait,' said his father. 'Stick close by me and don't get lost. They'll never take you on your own.'

Mr Harris then started to nudge and push his way forward in the crowd, with Moggy close in his wake. Being small they could slide into gaps unnoticed, so that they soon left Fred Keegan far behind. Sometimes the crowd of men heaved and Moggy felt that he was going to be suffocated. But his father never stopped inching forward at every opportunity and by 7.30 they were only three rows from the chain which held the men back from the dock gates.

The gates opened dead on time and half a dozen bowler-hatted supervisors emerged. Immediately there was a terrific noise as men shouted over each other, waving their cards and trying to catch a supervisor's eye. The supervisors for their part obviously enjoyed their position of power. They smiled as they looked over the crowd of jostling men – for all the world as the kids smiled in the playground of North Road School when they were chosen to 'pick up' teams for football. They used the same infuriating deliberation – stretching out the agony as long as possible. Slowly a little knot of men gathered behind each one.

'Curly Harris.'

'Here I am, Mr Jackson.'

'I thought you were on your knees down there.'

Mr Harris grabbed Moggy's hand and forced his way through to the front of the crowd.

'What's this you've got?' asked the supervisor, staring at Moggy.

'It's my lad. He left school yesterday.'

'What do you call him?'

'Moggy.'

'I thought a Moggy was a cat.'

'His real name's Morgan, but everyone calls him Moggy.'

'Looks like you, I'd say.' Mr Jackson looked Moggy up and down. 'About the right height.'

'It weren't the lodger, if that's what you mean,' replied Mr Harris with a laugh.

'But he's got straight hair.'

'Got to inherit something from his mum, ain't he?'

Moggy could see that the talk was all part of the supervisor's way of spinning out the process of selection.

'Can we do with a boy in the gang?' Mr Jackson yelled to the foreman. The man looked round to assess his team and then nodded. The supervisor, who had now had enough of the chat, indicated that they should take their place with the others.

As Mr Harris had predicted, it turned out to be a good day. By the time that the supervisors had finished putting their gangs together two thirds of the men had been taken on. Most of those left outside were casual labourers, strayed in from other jobs, who could only hope for work when the regular dockers were inside. Moggy did, however, see the burly figure of Fred Keegan still behind the chain when the last man had been taken on. That was an object lesson for him, declared his father. Fred was 'known' as a union trouble-maker and the supervisors ganged up to see that he did not get more than a couple of days' work a week. It only went to show that it was unwise to get too deeply involved.

Their gang was set to unload a cargo of jute from the hold of a tall-funnelled P & O merchantman. All through the day the men worked with a steady rhythm. Moggy could not have handled the bales for one hour – let alone twelve – but the men knew from experience just how much could be expected of a boy. Curly Harris protected his son, without ever appearing to do so.

Moggy did odd jobs, tying up bales that had come undone, fetching the men's sandwiches and cold tea, and taking his turn in the line when one of the men had to drop out. Most of the gang had worked together before and knew each other's ways. No one talked much, but every now and then one or other of them would throw some question or comment in Moggy's direction.

'At North Road, were you? Old Pender still there? He must be knocking on a bit. Hits hard for a little geezer, don't he? Reckon they spoiled a fair old docker when they made him a teacher.'

'Ever go down to watch West Ham? Play football yourself?'

'See that clipper? She's off to Shanghai.'

'Watch your head, mate. Your mum wouldn't like it if you lost it on the first day.'

Sometimes they asked his father the questions, getting in digs where they could.

'Has he got a bit of skirt to go home to?'

'Give him a chance. He's only fourteen.'

'I thought they started young these days. After all, he's big and handsome – like his dad.'

40

'Watch it!'

'Little and handsome, then. Anyway it's a load of cods-wallop about the tarts going for the big blokes. The most successful men are all small. The lad's got a great future.'

Occasionally Moggy would try to answer back for himself, but his speed of repartee was far behind that of the men. One or two of them seemed to enjoy getting one over on him, so after a few attempts he let his father do the talking for him. It soon became clear to Moggy that Curly Harris was a very different man at work from the one at home. When talking to his mates in the gang he had a confidence and a lightness of touch which Moggy had never seen before. He was, in fact, a more complete man on the wharf than he ever was at home.

After what seemed endless hours of labour the time for the dinner break arrived. For a moment Moggy hung back, uncertain whether to take his handkerchief into a corner on his own. But his father helped him over his indecision. Taking Moggy by the shoulder he propelled him forward into the main group. Sitting down on a bale of jute, he tugged at the knot on his handkerchief. He was ready for something to eat and the bread and meat tasted better than they ever had before. At first the men ate quietly. Then several of them lit up pipes or rolled thin cigarettes and began to chat.

Moggy was glad to stay out of the line of conversation. He was in no mood for defending himself or answering back. But, as he sat silently, he felt himself drawn into the group. It was only the day before that he had sung, 'O God our help in ages past.' Then he had been a kid at school. Now he was at work – the real thing. And at the end of the day he would be paid in real money. As the mid-day break drew to a close he flexed the life back into his tired muscles, ready to start work once again.

In the afternoon the coalies arrived to fill the ship's bunkers. The noise of their shovels made conversation difficult, and anyone who was foolish enough to open his mouth soon acquired a coating of fine black dust on

41

his tongue and throat. One or two of the dockies wrapped handkerchiefs round their faces; others worked with their lips tight shut. Moggy discovered that the coal dust found its way up his nostrils and under the lids of his eyes. As the afternoon wore on he watched his arms change colour as the dust lodged in the short hairs and dissolved in his sweat. Every now and again he cleared his mouth by spitting grey saliva on to the dock.

By five o'clock Moggy looked and felt like a docker. To his relief the coalies finished their work and gradually the air on the dockside cleared. The men began to speak one or two words, but they now kept their remarks pared down to essentials.

Moggy watched the hands of the clock on the wharf-side move imperceptibly towards half past five. As far as he was concerned the day could not end soon enough. Shortly before the shift was due to finish he noticed that the rhythm of the men was slowing down. At first he thought that they were tired at the end of the day. Then he noticed that unspoken messages passed from one to the other. Immediately the supervisor appeared round the corner of the wharf, however, the work rhythm resumed its normal pace.

'How are we going?' asked Mr Jackson. He clambered up the gangway and looked down into the hold. 'How much more?' he called.

Moggy could not hear the answer from down below. The men were standing, waiting for the verdict.

'Two hours overtime.'

Two hours overtime! The men looked tired, but they winked at each other before starting work again.

'All right, lad?' asked his father.

'All right.'

Moggy settled down to work, but the supervisor called to him. 'You kid, what's your name. Knock off now.'

'I can go on.'

'That's your lot, matey. Collect your money from the gate and beat it.'

42

None of the men – not even his father – turned to see Moggy go. As he walked alone along the long wharf his back ached and his legs were stiff. He reported, as instructed, to the paying office and received 5s 3d for his first day's work.

The walk back along the East India Dock Road and the Commercial Road seemed twice as long as it had in the morning. He stopped to buy a hot potato off an old woman with a brazier at the corner of the street. Other dockers were turning into the public houses which lined the streets. Moggy was more interested in the warmth of a cup of tea but he was afraid that, if he stopped at a café, he would not have the strength to start walking again. He was nearly home before he realized that he had earned enough during the day to justify paying the fare for a tram; in the Harris family only those who earned travelled in trams and Moggy had not yet picked up the habit.

None of the family asked him any questions about his day's work but Bet was sent to draw a bath of hot water from the copper in the scullery. When he was clean and rested his mother held her hand out. Moggy felt in his pocket and gave her 2s 6d. She checked the coins and shrugged. She had never succeeded in finding out how much her husband earned in a full day's work, and she made no attempt to question Moggy; 2s 6d was a handsome enough contribution to the family exchequer. In a fit of generosity Moggy took another sixpence and tossed it between Charlie and Bet.

'Share that between you,' he said. 'And get something for Doris.'

'Don't throw your money about,' said his mother.

'It's my first pay, ain't it?' he replied. 'I won't always get a full day.'

'All the more reason for saving your money, while you've got it. There'll come a time when you'll be glad of it.'

But Moggy had no intention of saving anything. He was

wondering whether the busy time would last long enough for him to collect the money needed to start training. He had no idea how much it would cost, but he had a nasty feeling that a proper gym would be beyond his resources for the time being. In any case he was much too tired to do anything about it that night.

3

There was no shortage of work at the docks for the rest of the week and Moggy was fit for nothing at the end of the day but to go home, have a bite to eat, sit about for a bit and get into bed. At least that way he did not spend much and, when work stopped at 3 o'clock on Saturday afternoon, his pocket felt heavy with the money he had earned.

As soon as he had washed and eaten he strolled out into the street to see whether he could come up with any of his friends from school. Bet wanted him to stop and play with her and, as he walked down Cable Street, he was followed by her whole crowd. Every now and again one would dart across his path and make him stumble.

'Push off,' growled Moggy.

'See you skip,' shouted a tall, scrawny child from the back. 'We'll call out for you.'

'I said, push off.'

'Give us a tanner for sweets then,' called Bet.

'I earned my money.'

'Oh, he's getting a big boy now.'

One girl jumped up and snatched the cap off his head. 'He's too posh to play with us,' she shouted. 'Catch.'

For a couple of minutes Moggy was an angry and undignified pig in the middle while the children tossed his cap from one to another. He retrieved it when one girl made the mistake of throwing it to Doris. The child made a good attempt to hold on to it, but Moggy wrenched it roughly from her hands, leaving her sitting, yelling on the pavement.

'Go find Lushy Sue,' he suggested. 'Plague the life out of her for a change.'

'We're bored,' replied Bet. 'There's nothing to do round here.'

'Give us a penny each for the flicks,' suggested one.

'You can go to the pictures when you can pay for yourselves. I ain't forking out for you. That's flat.'

The children sensed that they had pushed him far enough. As he strode on they made no attempt to follow. Moggy decided that he was most likely to find some of his friends around one or other of the markets. Being the closest, he went first to Watney Street. The market was going full swing as the costers knocked down their prices, step by step. The reductions were finely timed. The man who left it too late would have goods on his hands over the weekend. The one who reduced too early was in danger of cutting out all his profit. Children, holding large bags, stood by the stalls waiting to buy at the best possible moment. Moggy had learned the trick long ago. Fine timing was essential. He had kicked himself a few times when he bought at what he thought would be bottom price, only to hear the coster shouting an even lower one a few minutes later. But he had also hung back too long so that, by the time he got to the front of the queue, everything was sold out. He particularly remembered one disastrous occasion. His mother had cuffed his ear when he came in without any meat. The family had had to live on potato soup all weekend, and his father had cuffed his ear at every meal-time for good measure.

'Two penn'orth of cagmag.' A barefooted child held up two pence as Moggy had done so often in the past.

The butcher swept the ends of meat and offal into a piece of newspaper and handed it to the child. 'Here you are, governor,' he declared. 'Two pounds worth of the best sirloin. You'll find it lovely.' He looked over to Moggy and held up a sheep's heart. 'Have a nice heart. There you are.' He put two hearts on to a sheet of newspaper. 'Fourpence. You won't get it cheaper than that. Tell you the truth, I'm robbing myself. Charitable institution, that's what I'm becoming.' Moggy turned away and the butcher pushed the hearts under the nose of a passing woman. 'Fourpence . . . threepence ha'penny.'

'Threepence,' she bargained.

'You'll put me in the workhouse, lady,' he declared, wrapping them up swiftly. 'Threepence it is, then.'

Moggy picked his way through the debris which surrounded the next vegetable stall and paused to listen to the patter of the quack who was extolling the properties of his latest brand of medicine to a sceptical audience.

'Ladies and gentlemen,' he bellowed, 'have you got anything wrong with you? Indigestion perhaps? Liver out of order? Have you got twinges in the small of your back or spots before your eyes? I tell you that this wonderful medicine will bring instant relief for all disorders. Try a bottle; only a shilling. Let your friends know what it has done for you.'

As he turned from one to another his long black cloak billowed behind him and his beady eyes scanned the members of his audience as if they could diagnose their ailments at a glance.

'What's it made of, crocus?' shouted a voice at the back.

'Horse piss and pepper,' replied a fat woman at the front.

Her analysis was greeted with screams of delight. But the vendor ignored the distraction with a high disdain. He could afford to. Moggy knew that several of the women who joined in the laughter would slink back to buy a bottle when the crowds had dispersed. On his rare days of sickness his mother always dosed him with just such evil concoctions.

A man added to the merriment by belching loudly. This time the quack grabbed his opportunity. 'Did I hear a gentleman calling for a bottle? This medicine provides a miraculous cure for flatulence. If the gentleman will speak out again – '

Moggy admired the way that he had twisted the laughter to his own advantage. He supposed that selling coloured water was one way to make a living – a good deal easier

47

than heaving goods around in the docks – but he didn't fancy it himself.

'Mog!' Suddenly Moggy heard the voice of Jan Jaworski calling from the other side of the street. He had a shovel and had paused in the process of clearing up an unpleasant pile of refuse from the back of a poultry stall. Moggy was not sure whether to answer, but the Pole shouted again and walked over towards him.

'Been working?' asked Jan.

'If you'd call it work,' replied Moggy.

'Docks?'

Moggy nodded. 'You been doing anything?'

Jaworski looked down at his shovel and shrugged. 'Odd jobs.'

For a moment it seemed as though the conversation had petered out for good. They stood in silence watching the quack doctor pass off several bottles of his medicine to bashful-looking women.

'Anything on tonight?' asked Jan.

'I hadn't thought,' replied Moggy, uncertain about committing himself.

'Come up the Mile End Road.'

'Just you and me?' Moggy was not keen on some of the kids who had hung around with Jan at school.

'We'll start that way anyway. Got any spandulicks?' asked Jan.

'A bit.'

'I'll have one and six when this geezer's paid me. Wait until I finish shovelling this muck.' Jan looked down at the piled mass of fat, heads, legs and intestines without emotion. 'Ten minutes. Don't run away.'

'Ten minutes,' confirmed Moggy. 'I'll be back.'

He strolled off round the market. The butcher had sold his last scraps, and was wiping down his stall, but the quack was still in full spate, going through his routine for a new set of customers. For a wild moment Moggy was tempted to buy a bottle of the magic brew to cure the selection of aches and pains which were the legacy of four

48

days' work. Casting this idea swiftly behind him, he tried to see what the effect would be of belching as loudly as he could from the back of the crowd, but he was unable to produce a sound loud enough to be heard.

In rather under ten minutes he was back at the poulterer's chewing a perfectly good apple which he had found lying on the refuse by the vegetable stall. Jan had finished his job and was collecting a couple of coppers from the stall holder.

When he was ready they set off together, picking their way between the stalls. Those costers who had not packed up were shouting out with redoubled vigour.

'Last pound of carrots, lady.'

'Fish. All alive-o.'

'Have you got indigestion? Liver out of order –'

'Don't he ever give up?' asked Moggy.

'Not till they've all gone home. I'm sick of listening to him. It's a load of balls.'

Moggy attempted a last belch as he walked past, but again he failed miserably. After they had left the noise of the market behind them they began to exchange news of the week. Jan had to agree that Moggy had done well enough. He refused to budge from his position, however; anyone who went to work in the docks of his own free will needed his head examined. For his part, he had picked up a few odd jobs labouring round the ships and the market, but it was clear to Moggy that 1s 6d in his pocket represented almost everything that he had earned. Nevertheless he was obviously set on spending it that evening.

They walked along the Commercial Road, and then cut north along the canal, making for the Mile End Road. Moggy suggested that they should start by getting a bite to eat. Although Jan agreed that he could do with something, none of the cafés which they passed suited him. One glance inside seemed enough to put him off. They had reached the Mile End Road before he found one which caught his fancy. Moggy could not see what it had over the others until Jan dug him in the ribs and nodded towards two girls sitting at a table in the corner.

'Fancy one?' asked Jan.

Moggy thought that they were probably young enough to be still at school, but they had got themselves up for an evening out. The colour on their thin faces seemed rather more vivid than that provided by nature alone.

'I'm ready for a bite anyway,' replied Moggy, going in through the door of the café.

When they had collected a pie and chips and a cup of tea, Jan steered Moggy to the table next to the girls. He could tell from their faces that they had not missed the significance of the manœuvre. At first Jan seemed to pay no attention to them. He cut into the pie and ate one mouthful before reaching for the sauce. The bottle was conveniently empty. Nodding at Moggy he turned to the girl nearest to him on the next table.

'Got any sauce, darling?' he asked.

'Hark at him! Seems he's got enough sauce to be getting on with, don't you think?' The two girls giggled at one another as they handed over the bottle.

Jan sprinkled the sauce over his pie and took several mouthfuls at a leisurely pace before renewing the conversation. 'Live round here?' he asked.

'Not far,' replied the girl nearest him.

'What do you do?'

The girls exchanged a swift glance. 'We work in a shop.'

From their expression Moggy was more certain than ever that they were still at school.

'Harrods?' asked Jan.

The girls laughed at each other. 'Don't be daft. What do you do?' The question was directed at both of them, but Moggy realized that Jan had chosen his seat with care and the dialogue lay between him and the girl nearest him. Moggy and her friend were so far just passengers.

Jan nodded at Moggy. 'He's a docker.'

'I'm going to be a boxer.' Moggy regretted his boast as

soon as he had opened his mouth. In the first place it was hardly true; he had not even started training and he had intended to say nothing to anybody until he had proved to himself that he could do it. In the short term, however, it did succeed in drawing him into the picture. The second girl began to look at him with considerably greater interest.

Jan took the cue without batting an eyelid. 'Should do well. He's a tough little bloke. You don't want to get on the wrong side of this lad.'

'What's your names?' asked Jan's girl.

'I'm Jan. He's Moggy.'

'Moggy? That can't be your name.'

'What's wrong with it? You'll see it at the top of the bill one day.' Jan drew the name in the air with his hand.

The girl who was sitting next to Jan showed remarkably little interest in Moggy's ambitions – or indeed in Moggy. She looked at Jan. 'What about you?'

'I'm putting in time.'

'What're you waiting for?' she retorted. 'Christmas?'

'I'm going to join the army,' replied Jan.

She studied him intently for a moment. 'You ain't English,' she announced at last.

'How can you tell?' asked Moggy. 'He speaks all right.'

The girl continued to ignore Moggy. 'It's your face,' she said. 'Russian?'

'Not far out,' replied Jan. 'Polish.'

'What's your name?'

'I told you. Jan.'

'Don't they give you two names in Poland, then?'

'Jaworski,' he replied uncertainly. 'They all just calls me Jan.'

'Jaworski,' she said. 'Nothing wrong with that. Can you speak Polish?'

'We do at home.'

'Go on,' urged the girl. 'Say something in Polish for us.'

Jan had obviously had enough of the conversation and started playing with the food on his plate. The other girl butted in quickly to cover his embarrassment.

'I'm Clara,' she announced. 'She's Vicky. Are you friends?'

Moggy looked at Jan. 'Sort of.'

'Vicky and I goes around together, don't we, Vic?'

'Like that, is it?' said Moggy. 'Can't tell t'other from which?'

'You'll learn quick enough,' put in Vicky sharply.

Jan finished toying with his pie and looked up at Vicky. 'What're you doing tonight?' he asked.

The girl turned round to her friend. 'We hadn't thought, had we, Clara?'

'Moggy and I was going to the Paragon, wasn't we, Mog?'

It was the first that Moggy had heard of it but he saw no reason to disagree.

Vicky obviously had a practical turn of mind. 'We ain't got no money,' she warned him quickly.

'We wasn't expecting you to pay. Moggy's in the ackers. I tell you, he's a working man. Generous too.' Seeing that Moggy did not appreciate the joke, Jan added. 'I've got enough for the gods myself.'

'When does it start?' asked Clara.

'There's plenty of time,' Jan assured her. 'Give us a chance.'

'Feeding time at the zoo,' said Vicky. 'Watch the animals eat.'

'You needn't look, if you don't want to,' said Jan. 'Go and get more for yourselves.'

The two girls obviously thought that that was not too bad an idea; they looked across at Moggy as the one in the ackers. But, having no intention of turning out money at such an early stage in the evening, Moggy directed all his attention at the plate of pie and chips in front of him.

There were nights when Moggy felt like being entertained, and nights when he did not. Left to himself he would never have chosen that evening for a visit to the music hall. The thick atmosphere made him feel sleepy and his muscles began to ache with fatigue.

His mind was much more taken up with his own immediate problem than with what was happening on the stage. Before that evening he had thought about being a boxer but, since he had told nobody about his plans, he could afford to take his time – or even drop the idea altogether if he wanted. Now that he had opened his mouth, if he was not going to look a prize idiot, he had to do something about it. The problem was that Moggy had not the first idea of how to get started on a career in the ring. The solution came to him when, in a shaft of inspiration, he remembered that Bet's friend, Liz, had an uncle who had been a pug. Although he had retired he would still have contacts in the fight world. Moggy decided that he would not delay any longer. It would be no problem to find Liz, and, since it was Sunday next day, she would be able to take him to her uncle.

Once he had solved his problem Moggy tried to bring his mind back to the show. Being Saturday night the house was full and Moggy was jammed tight between Clara on one side and Jan on the other. Vicky had taken advantage of the crush to drape herself round Jan's shoulders. The two of them were completely with the show. Vicky was laughing in a loud, high-pitched way, which Moggy thought must have been heard across the theatre. On his other side Clara managed to keep her distance so that their legs did not quite touch. Moggy thought that it was odd the way that girls always chose friends who were opposite to themselves in almost every way. Even when the funny man was making the audience rock with laughter, Clara's face hardly cracked in a smile. Moggy could not make out whether she was bored or whether it was just her manner.

The audience was in a receptive mood, and for the most part the artists had a good reception. Most of the songs were well known and when the audience joined in the choruses, Vicky and Jan more than made up for the fact that Moggy and Clara hardly sang at all.

The management must have been well enough pleased with the way that the evening was going until the moment that the master of ceremonies announced that he was introducing an exciting new artist to sing to them, and a pale looking girl in a billowy dress walked stiffly on to the stage. Experienced performers knew that they had to look their audience straight in the eye but, as the musicians played the introductory bars of her song, the girl stared first at the ceiling and then down at her feet. As she drew in her breath to sign she clenched her hands in front of her.

Moggy could have named half a dozen artists who could have got away with singing the sort of rubbish the girl had chosen. Knowing that she had to get herself across as quickly as possible she tried to wring all the sentiment out of the sickly words. The audience gave her just one verse to show what she could do before they started to laugh. Jan started the real barracking before she had finished the second verse.

'Off, off, off,' he shouted.

Soon the whole gallery had taken up his rhythmic chant. Moggy expected the girl to break down and run off, but she only clenched her hands tighter together as she tried to dredge yet more sentiment out of her song.

By the third verse Jan was on his feet, hurling his hard won pennies on to the stage. The rhythmic chant had broken and the audience was jeering mercilessly. Moggy thrust his hand into his pocket and took a grip of his money. If Jan wanted to throw his coppers away, he was not going to scrounge any off him when the show was over.

As the singer drew breath for the fourth verse Moggy wondered how any human being could stand such humiliation. He thought he detected a sob in her voice as, with hands clasped and eyes screwed up, and with the pennies dropping on to the stage around her, she struggled to the end of her stupid song. When she finished she bowed hurriedly and disappeared into the wings.

'Don't you feel for her?' asked Clara.

'Deserves all she gets,' replied Moggy uncharitably.

As he spoke the singer returned for a curtain call. The audience was astonished at her temerity.

'Get off,' yelled Jan. 'Off, off, off.'

But most of the gallery decided that the time had come to give her a bit of encouragement and they cheered as she bowed. Moggy reflected that crowds liked a good loser, in the ring or on the stage. But he had no intention of being a good loser. He wanted to win. The girl bowed a second time. She was going out well, but she had lost. The management would never take her on again. A couple more performances like that and no management in London would take her on ever again. She could then resign herself to spending the rest of her life sewing hats or wiping babies' bottoms. Even Jan was cheering as she bowed for the third and last time. Moggy wondered how she felt. Did she feel sick inside because they had given her the bird, or was she kidding herself that it would be better next time; that, with a bit of luck, she could still be another Marie Lloyd? It did not matter. She had lost either way.

Moggy was bored by the rest of the show and was glad when it was over. He kept close to Clara as they pushed their way through the exit and into the street. Once outside they looked round for the other two.

'They've hopped it,' announced Moggy at last.

Clara seemed genuinely put out at being abandoned by her friend. 'If they don't want our company – '

Moggy was more surprised that Jan had decided to do without his extra financial resources. 'Didn't you see them in there?' he said. 'They were as thick as two Jews on pay day.'

'No accounting for taste, I suppose,' announced Clara cryptically. Moggy wondered what she meant. Perhaps she wondered what Vicky saw in Jan, but that seemed improbable. Moggy was detached enough to realize that

– boxer or no – he was the natural second choice of the two. That meant that she could not understand why Jan preferred Vicky to her.

'Depends what you're looking for, don't it?' he replied, equally cryptically. 'Want some supper?'

'It's up to you,' she replied.

'Don't force yourself,' retorted Moggy.

She did not answer, but led the way up the broad Mile End Road. They walked in silence as neither of them could think of anything to talk about.

'What does your dad do?' asked Moggy at last.

'Chairman of the Board, ain't he?'

'No, straight up?'

'I ain't got a dad.'

'Skipped it, has he?' asked Moggy.

'He's dead. Happens to all of us sometime.' Hurriedly she changed the subject. 'Is it true what you said?'

'What's that?'

'About being a pug.'

'I ain't really started yet,' confessed Moggy. 'But I'm going to.'

'You ain't a proper professional, then?'

'Half a chance. I only just left school. I've got to fight as a boy first. It ain't that bad, though. You win proper money, even as a boy.'

'Enough to live on?'

'No, I suppose not. I'll go on working down the docks till I can be a pro.'

'You ain't going to be a dockie all your life, then?'

'Christ, no!' replied Moggy. Then he added, more realistically: 'It depends, really, don't it. I mean, you can't be a pro unless you're good enough.'

'I ain't never been to boxing,' said Clara. 'What's it like?'

'You'll have to find out for yourself, won't you. Do you like the sight of blood?'

'Don't mind.'

'My nose bleeds easy,' said Moggy. 'Will you come and

56

watch me when I get a proper fight?'

'I might. See how it takes me.' She walked on for a few paces before deciding to make her own confession. 'Vicky and me; we do work in a shop in the holidays.'

'Which school are you at?' asked Moggy.

'Monza Street. Bloody dump. We've got another year to do. I want to earn my own money.' She stopped and pointed to a green creation in the window of a dress shop. 'What do you think of that?'

'Horrible,' replied Moggy.

'What's wrong with it?'

'It'd be all right on a tart.'

Clara looked down at her own dress. It fitted her well enough but the colours had faded and Moggy could tell from the lines above the hem that it had been taken up and down a few times. It had either belonged to an elder sister or had been bought second hand.

When they went into a café and sat down to eat Clara found her tongue. She chattered about the clothes that she would buy when she had money of her own, and of the way that she would wear them to the West End. She conjectured about the kind of job that she was most likely to find when she left school in a year's time. Then she talked about the show which they had seen at the Paragon which apparently she had enjoyed from beginning to end.

Moggy found it easier to let her do the talking and to confine himself to plying her with food and drink to keep her going. If Clara had picked him because Vicky left her with no choice, she did not seem to regret it, and at the end of the evening she assumed that they would meet again. As he walked home, Moggy decided that the evening had turned out better than he had expected. Clara had enjoyed herself, and Moggy had managed to keep five shillings in his pocket to give him a start to his training.

Early on Sunday afternoon Liz took Moggy round to see

her uncle, whose name was Bob Tranter. The ex-professional was hardly an advertisement for the sport. Hundreds of punches, landed over the course of a long career, had pushed his nose backwards, and spread it outwards — rather more to the right than to the left. In the front room of the tiny house where he lived with his wife there were the photographs and trophies of his active days, but it was obvious from the way they lived that, if he had ever made any money out of boxing, he had not managed to hang on to it.

Liz took it on herself to explain that Moggy had been the toughest boy of his age at North Road School, and now he wanted proper boxing lessons. Bob Tranter explained that there were clubs where youngsters could learn the rudiments of the game. But, as he looked Moggy up and down, a better idea came to him. Ever since leaving the ring he had had ideas of taking up training. He had no premises, except his own back yard, but, if it suited Moggy, Bob was prepared to take him on as his first pupil. Then, if all went well, he would become his manager as well. Moggy had no hesitation in accepting the offer, and he paid over his five shillings on account. Bob Tranter took it gladly, but he refused to agree on a fee for lessons. That was to be fixed at some unspecified later date. In the meantime, Moggy could give him what he could, when he could.

For the next month Moggy hardly had any time to himself. Work continued brisk at the docks so that within a short time he was able to kit himself out with gloves, singlet and shorts. On some days work finished too late for him even to think of training, but at weekends, and on those days when work finished in reasonable time, he lost no time in getting round to Bob Tranter's house.

Within two weeks his teacher had delivered the judgement that Moggy was a born fighter. His style was certainly clumsy but he had any amount of courage. Even when the ex-professional let fly with a two-fisted barrage, Moggy would keep coming forward at him, looking for a way to land his own blow. It was as if he did not know how to retreat. In the course of time he learnt to dodge and parry the most dangerous of Bob's blows, and get a few of his own on target.

At the end of the month Tranter announced that he was going to take the plunge and put his man in the ring. By pulling some of his contracts he had managed to get him a spot on the bill at Premierland on the following Sunday. Moggy's stomach turned over when he heard the news. He had sat in the crowd watching the fighting at Premierland on several Sunday afternoons, and it had never occurred to him that one day his turn would come to be out there in the middle.

During those early weeks of training Moggy and Clara established the habit of meeting on Saturday nights. From time to time Clara hinted that most boys were prepared to spend a great deal more time and money on their girl friends than he was, but gradually she learned where she came in Moggy's order of priorities. His week-day evenings and most of his money were dedicated to boxing. If she could not make do with what was left, then she could do the other thing. Although she grumbled, the arrangement suited her quite well. She was not really looking for a grand love affair and at least Moggy made no demands on her, even if he did not give her much either.

The night before the fight Moggy met Clara as usual. For the first hour or so that they were together she could scarcely prise so much as a word out of him. Then at last, as they lingered over a cup of tea in a café, Moggy got round to talking about the match.

'You said you might come and watch me in the ring.'

Clara perked up and looked at him across the café table. 'What? Got a fight, have you?'

'I'm first on the bill at Premierland tomorrow.'

'First,' she said astounded. 'Do you mean top of the bill?'

'Turn it upside down and you'd be right.'

'Well, it's the right place to start, ain't it? Who're you fighting?'

'I don't know. Bob didn't tell me. Some kid.' Moggy looked down into his cup. 'You don't have to come.'

'Well, I ain't got anything better to do, have I? Who else is coming?'

'I ain't told nobody.'

Clara gave a yelp of astonishment. 'You right faggot. Why ever not —'

'I might make a fool of myself.' Clara was looking at him with mocking eyes so Moggy busied himself, stirring sugar into his tea, while he tried to make her understand. 'That singer at the Paragon; I'll bet she wished she hadn't brought her friends along that night we was there.'

'You're barmy,' said Clara. 'They've all got to know some time.'

'After the fight, all right. It's just I don't want them all there, laughing their socks off, while I'm getting bashed into kingdom come.'

'But you don't mind me?' asked Clara.

'You wouldn't laugh. You didn't laugh at that stupid singer.'

'Don't be so bleeding miserable, Moggy,' said Clara. 'You ain't going to lose. Jan said you was good.'

'I'm all right in a punch-up, but it's different in the ring. You can't use your trotter-cases for a start. Hell, I've only been learning how to box for a month.'

'Bob Tranter wouldn't have put you in for it if he didn't think you could win, would he?'

Clara's encouragement did Moggy good and, by the time that they split up for the night, he was feeling a good deal more confident. The last thing that they did was to arrange a time and place to meet so that they could walk to Premierland together in good time for the fight.

In point of fact Moggy found that he was to have a bigger following than he had bargained for. Liz heard about the fight from her Uncle Bob and passed on the news to Bet. Half a dozen of their gang managed to borrow or scrounge enough money to pay for entrance to the hall. All morning Bet and Charlie could speak of nothing but the fight and their enthusiasm soon set Moggy on edge. Mrs Harris put her foot down at the very idea that Doris might go with the older children. The child screamed, pouted and whimpered by turns for the next hour and a half in a vain attempt to make her change her mind. By the end of the morning Moggy felt that he was going crazy. Even before the fight began, his body started to ache in a dozen places. Some were genuine aches, where muscles grumbled at the sacks and cases that he had humped about the wharf in the past weeks. Some were just aches in places which he expected to be hit before the day was over.

His mother insisted that he could not fight on an empty stomach and so he was sat down before a bowl of stew and made to eat it up before he was allowed to leave the house. When at last he set off for Premierland he was accompanied by a large retinue. Charlie walked alongside him and Bet's mob followed behind.

Clara was waiting at the corner of the Commercial Road ten minutes before the time they had arranged to meet.

'I thought that lot weren't coming,' she said drily as he came up to her.

'I didn't tell them,' protested Moggy.

Bet ran forward and examined Clara. 'Who's this?' she demanded.

'Friend of mine,' replied Moggy sharply.

'What else have you got to hide, Mog?' jeered Bet. 'Didn't tell us he'd got a fight. Didn't tell us about the girl friend. Where did you pick her up?' Moggy took a swing at her, but she ducked out of range.

Clara straightened her dress round her thighs and set off along the road with her head held high. Moggy ran a few paces to catch her up.

'You're coming?' he asked.

61

'Perhaps I've changed my mind. I ain't going to put up with her cheek.'

'Where are you going then?'

She put on her most sarcastic voice. 'There and back to see how far it is.'

'Suit yourself,' replied Moggy.

Once Clara had made her protest it became obvious that she had no serious intention of missing the fight. Before long she was talking about the prospects and she even deigned to speak to Bet. The group trudged on towards Premierland, keeping to the centre of the road all the way and making a lot of noise for Sunday dinner time. Moggy felt like their champion as he walked with his gloves slung over his shoulder and his kit hitched under his arm. It seemed right now that he should have a following for his first fight.

'Competitor,' announced Moggy when he reached the turnstiles.

The attendant looked at him without interest and jerked his thumb to the side. 'Round the back. Next.' He held out his hand for Clara's money.

'I'll pay for you,' said Moggy, reaching into his pocket.

'There's love for you,' jeered Bet. 'He never forks out for me.'

'Shut your teeth, can't you,' growled Moggy as he turned to follow the direction of the attendant's thumb.

'Good luck, Mog,' called Charlie after him. 'See you clobber him good and proper.'

Moggy waved his gloves in the air without turning round and stumped off towards the competitors' entrance. He now had a sinking feeling in the pit of his stomach. He wondered whether he was mad to fight with so little training behind him. But he reassured himself that Bob Tranter would not have let him into the ring if he had thought that he was going to make a fool of himself.

'Competitor,' said Moggy to the attendant on the back door.

'Name?'

'Harris.'

The man checked down the list on his board. 'First fight. You've got half an hour. Get changed; then wait till you're called.'

The changing room was deserted except for one lad who was already in his kit and was standing uncertainly at the far end. Moggy chose the opposite corner and tried to size the other up as he slipped his shirt over his head. At first he thought that the lad could not be his opponent, since he was a good six inches taller. But he had a slim body which could not have weighed much, so in the end he decided that they were not as unequal as appeared at first sight. Moggy made no attempt to speak as he changed into his new kit.

'First fight?' asked the other lad at last.

'That's right. You too?'

The other boy nodded and the conversation ended. They sat in their corners as the changing room gradually began to fill up with a number of other fighters – most of them little older than they were.

At last an attendant in a large white sweater came to the door. 'Jim Gates. Moggy Harris,' he called. The two of them walked towards him. 'Long and the short of it, eh?' he remarked as he looked from one to the other. 'Feeling fit? Follow me.'

He led them into the side room and motioned Gates on to the scales. 'Eight stone, three pounds,' he said. 'Now you, nipper.' When Moggy got on the scales the attendant moved the weight on the arm backwards, but then realized that he had got it wrong. 'You're heavier than you look,' he remarked as he slid it outwards again. 'Eight stone, six pounds. Grow a bit and we'll have you fighting heavy weight.' The attendant checked his watch and waited for a couple of minutes. 'Let's see your gloves, lads,' he said at last. He checked them and then helped them put them on. 'First time?' he asked. Both lads nodded. 'Don't be scared. Just fight as if nobody was watching.' He beckoned them to follow him and they walked out into the main hall.

If Moggy was afraid of fighting in front of a big crowd, he need not have worried. By the time that the main fights came on, later in the afternoon, the hall would be full, with people standing round the back. But now, at two o'clock, it was more than two thirds empty. A steady stream of spectators were coming in but not many of them paid any attention to the two boys as they ducked under the ropes. Only the small knot of their devoted followers yelled and cheered. Most of the noise came from his opponent's corner, and Moggy was glad that Bet and Charlie had come with their friends as Clara would not have made much of a showing on her own – she was not really the yelling type.

'Ladies and gentlemen,' announced the M.C. 'The first fight of the afternoon. A novice contest. In the red corner: Jim Gates of New Cross. Weight eight stone, three pounds. In the blue corner: Moggy Harris of Wapping. Eight stone, six pounds. A contest in five rounds.'

Bet led the shouting from the blue corner as the two lads walked out into the middle. Before they closed Moggy repeated Bob Tranter's final advice on him: 'Don't worry about the fancy stuff. Fight it your own way.'

Both boys threw their left hands at the same time, but Gates had several inches' advantage in reach and his landed squarely on Moggy's mouth, while Moggy's own blow petered out harmlessly in mid-air. The taller lad danced away and then circled round, looking for another opening.

Moggy kept on following, in his slow, flat-footed style, but he could never get within range to land a respectable blow. Time after time, through the first round, Gates's long left hand jabbed out to Moggy's face, and by the end of the round his nose had started to bleed.

After a couple of minutes even Bet was losing heart. Above the loud encouragement coming from the red corner, Moggy could hear the odd shout from the main body of the hall.

'Stop the fight, ref. Let's have the next.'

'Go home and grow up, little-un.'

By the end of the round Jim Gates was smiling in a way that reminded Moggy of Jan Jaworski. When the bell rang Moggy wiped the blood from his lip with the back of his glove and walked back to his corner.

'Sorry I'm late, kid.' Bob Tranter was standing waiting for him. Moggy could tell from the pained expression on his face that he had a monumental hangover.

'Did you see it?' asked Moggy.

'Nearly all. You're going to beat him, kid.'

'I ain't hit him yet.'

Bob wrung out the sponge and wiped his boxer's face. 'But he's hit you. He's given you all he's got and that ain't much.' Moggy wiped his nose again on his arm and looked at the red smear. 'Don't worry about a bit of blood. He can't hit. You can. Keep going at him. When you see a chance, get under his guard. Cut out the fancy stuff. Just hit him. Like I showed you, remember?'

The bell rang and the two boxers walked out again into the middle of the ring. Moggy crouched low and tucked his head on to his chest, so that the difference in height became even more pronounced. Gates obviously had instructions to step up the pace of his attack and finish the bout off. As he came in on a two-fisted assault he left his body unguarded for the first time. Moggy ducked under the left and took a sharp blow from the right as he plunged forward for his first real assault.

By the time that his opponent disentangled himself from the flying arms he had taken the best part of a dozen blows to the body. The blue corner came alight once again. Bet was now going mad with delight. Even Clara was on her feet.

'Hit him, Moggy. Hit him.'

Moggy did not let his man off the hook. Again and again he drove his way through the taller boy's blows until he

D. 65 C

could work at close quarters. The hall fell quiet, except for the shouts of encouragement, and some of the latecomers stood watching from the gangways.

'You've got him,' yelled Bet, almost beside herself. 'Do for him.'

'To the face; to the face,' shouted Bob from the corner.

Moggy coiled himself up for a blow to his opponent's undefended chin but he was beaten by the bell.

'There's my fighter,' declared Bob Tranter as he walked back into the corner. 'You've got him groggy. Next round you can finish him off.' Bob went on talking, but Moggy did not listen to what he said. He was impatient to get into the middle again. He was already on his feet before the bell rang.

It took only one minute of the round for Moggy to end the fight. The first solid punch to the chin sent Jim Gates down on to the canvas. He could have beaten the count, but Moggy was standing with his fists up, waiting for him, and the lad had obviously had enough.

'The winner. Moggy Harris of Wapping,' shouted out the referee as he held up his right hand. The sparse audience clapped as Moggy waved to the kids at his corner.

'I'll make a boxer of you,' declared Bob Tranter. 'You've got it, boy. You've got what it takes.'

'He didn't want no more, did he?' said Moggy with a grin.

'I ain't surprised. You've got a punch, boy.'

The contestant for the next bout was waiting by the corner so Moggy ducked under the ropes. The win was worth three shillings to him. One day, he felt sure, he would fight later in the programme when the hall was full. Perhaps he would even be top of the bill and pick up the thirty guinea prize which was offered on the hoardings. It would be a lot better than slaving his guts out for a few bob a day as a dockie. But it was no good being impatient. Everything took time and he was not fifteen yet.

4

The bad time started on the first Monday in June. Moggy woke early to hear the rain beating on the pavements outside. He knew well enough what the rain would mean. None of the ships with perishable cargoes would unload and only a lucky few would get work. Since it was already light, he slipped on his trousers and jacket and ran upstairs to wake his father.

'Rain!' he whispered, shaking him roughly.

'Eh? What?'

'Rain! It's pissing down.'

Mr Harris sat up in bed beside his sleeping wife and listened. 'That's heavy,' he growled. He had to make a decision. They could give up the idea of work and sleep in; if the rain stopped before the second call, they might get taken on later in the day. Alternatively, they could make an early start so as to get front places at the dock gate. A few men got work even on such a morning. Since they were awake it was worth a try.

'Stir yourself, woman,' he said, giving his wife a dig in the back. 'Make some hot tea.'

'What time is it?'

'Don't fuss about the time. Just do what I say.'

'Keep your bleeding voice down,' she complained. 'You'll wake the baby. He's been yelling half the night. Not that you'd know.'

She heaved reluctantly out of bed and padded downstairs. Within ten minutes Mr Harris had shaved and the tea was on the table. It was only half past five when he and Moggy grabbed a couple of sacks each – one for the head and one for the shoulders – from a grubby looking pile which lay in a corner of the room, and stepped out into the rain. Moggy did not know when he had ever seen rain coming down so hard. The water bounced off the pavement and streams of filthy water washed along the gulleys.

'Where to?' asked Moggy.

'Surrey Docks,' replied his father.

'For Christ's sake,' grumbled Moggy.

'What's up? At least you'll walk dry some of the way.'

By the time they reached the mouth of the Blackwall tunnel the rain had already penetrated the sacking and Moggy could feel the damp seep down the back of his neck. As soon as they were safely in the dry of the tunnel Curly Harris shook out both his sacks and wiped his face. A few other men were walking along the pavement and a cart lumbered slowly along the roadway from the Surrey side.

'Wet enough for you?' called the driver cheerfully.

'Get out there and find out,' replied Mr Harris.

It was still dark in the middle of the tunnel and water dripped endlessly off the damp walls, as if in imitation of the downpour outside. The sky on the south side looked dark for a June morning and Moggy and his father wrapped up again in their wet sacking before they ventured out into the open. Without a breath of wind the surface of the Thames was pocked only by the innumerable droplets of rain. The smoke from half a dozen factory chimneys fell downwards over the roofs before settling as a fine film of white over the surface of the river.

They had hoped that most of the dockers had decided to give first call a miss, but by the time that they arrived, a good crowd of sodden men were already huddled in at the Surrey Dock gate. The front two rows were packed tight and those already there had no intention of giving way. Everyone was soaked to the skin and few bothered any more to protect themselves with the sacking or pieces of water-proofing which they had brought with them as they waited in silence for the supervisors to appear.

In time more men came and packed tight behind, so that Moggy found himself jammed in a mass of wet, ill-tempered humanity. He could only see the back of the man immediately in front of him and feel the water pour from the brim of his saturated cap. The wait seemed endless. By the time that the supervisors were due to appear the crowd had grown to about two thirds of the size it would have been on a dry morning. Although they were well placed in the front, Moggy knew that the chance of their getting any work was remote. Those behind had certainly had a soaking for nothing. But they stayed.

The supervisors chose that morning to be late. The men grumbled that they had obviously taken one look at the rain and gone to sleep again, but Moggy thought that they were spinning out the agony. It was just the sort of thing that they would do. Teachers could do the same sort of thing when they felt like it.

At last the crowd gave a great lurch forward. Although Moggy could see nothing he knew that the supervisors must have arrived. Having turned out on such a morning, the men were all determined to get work if humanly possible. Fists flew as they fought one another for the best positions. One man near Moggy was even waving his cargo-hook dangerously in the air.

'Stand still, Moggy. Stand still, I tell you.' Curly Harris had worked his way behind his son and was trying to climb on to his back. 'Catch my foot and heave.'

Moggy almost choked as his father grasped him round the neck and he groped blindly for the boot which was scraping up and down his side.

'Get hold of it, can't you? Pull me up.' Curly Harris's voice rose to a shrill scream as he shouted over the noise.

'I'm trying, ain't I?' snapped Moggy. At last he managed to get his hand under the sole of his father's boot and he heaved as hard as he could. His father scrambled upwards, pressing down with one hand on the top of his son's head.

'Mr Richmond, governor. Curly Harris. You know me. I've worked for you.' As he shouted he waved his cap, spraying even more water over the surrounding crowd.

'Governor. You know me.' Mr Harris tried to work his

way forward on to the back of the next man, but his hand was brusquely knocked away. 'Mr Richmond.'

'You.' Immediately the supervisor's finger pointed in his direction Curly Harris jumped off his son's back. Grabbing Moggy by the wrist, he drove his way to the front of the crowd.

'Curly Harris,' he reported breathlessly.

Mr Richmond nodded him to join the bedraggled group of men who were standing apart. Moggy followed his father for a few steps before the supervisor called him back.

'Who are you?'

'Moggy Harris.'

'Hop it.'

'I'm his son,' protested Moggy.

'I don't care if you're the Emperor of China. I said hop it.'

Less than a quarter of the men had found work. The rest broke up into little knots and walked dejectedly away. The rain was coming down, though not as hard as before, and the men craned their necks, scanning the sky for any sign of a break in the clouds.

'Rain before seven, fine before eleven,' announced one prophet hopefully. At that moment a gust of wind brought it down even more heavily.

'What do you bet?' asked his mate.

'Tanner.'

'You're on.'

'Back here at eleven o'clock for second call, then,' replied the first. 'Have your money ready.'

Moggy did not know whether it was worth waiting. There was a lot to be said for calling it a day and going home. But he only had a few coppers left in his pocket. He invested one of them in two large chunks of white bread and propped himself up in the dry of a doorway to eat his way through them while he thought the problem over.

'Moggy Harris, isn't it?'

He looked up and saw that he was sharing the doorway with Fred Keegan, the union man. 'Yeah.' Moggy took another bite and shook the rain out of his cap.

'Curly get work, then?'

Moggy nodded.

'Lucky bastard. How did he do it?'

'By climbing on my perishing back. That's how. Yelling blue murder, he was.'

'Degrading.'

'Look, mister! He got work. That's more than you did.' Moggy tore off a huge lump of bread and crammed it into his mouth.

'I'm not blaming Curly. It's the system. Treat dockers like blooming slaves. Just because it's raining the bosses reckon we don't have to eat.'

Moggy's mouth was too full for comment, but he held out the second piece of bread. Fred Keegan shook his head once but, when Moggy did not retract his offer, he broke it in half and nodded his thanks.

'Got kids, have you?' asked Moggy at last.

'Three girls. Take a bit of feeding.'

'They'd eat a damned sight better if you didn't muck about with the union.'

'That's my business,' replied Keegan sharply.

'I should have thought that it was their business and all.'

'Someone's got to do it.'

'Catch me. Do you ever work?'

Fred Keegan paused for a moment before replying. 'Two – three days a week. We don't starve.'

'Stuff that for a way to live,' announced Moggy.

'You're your father's son, no mistake. Can't see further than the end of your wet nose. And you'll be back at the dock gates tomorrow, ready to take anything they hand out to you. Climbing on one another's backs like animals.'

'What else can you do when all you can see is the next geezer's shoulders? The supervisor ain't going to know there's a short-arsed Harris in the back row, is he?'

'I'm not getting at you, mate,' Fred reassured him. 'But to hell with a job where a little bloke has to fight to be seen.'

'Life's like that, ain't it?' declared Moggy. 'Just means you've got to fight harder.'

'It doesn't have to be like that. Look, Moggy; dockers could have steady employment, like blokes in other jobs.'

'If there's more ships in they need more men. If the work ain't there, there ain't nothing you can do about it. Stands to reason.'

'Then they've bloody well got to organize it so that there's always work. Even when it's raining.'

'See them do that.'

'There's no reason why not. Look, kid, it was different when they were all sailing ships. If the wind blew in the wrong direction there weren't much anyone could do about it. When the wind turned they all arrived together. But they've invented steam you know.'

'Get away!'

'Ships work to schedules – like buses. It isn't beyond the wit of man to organize the schedules so they get spaced out.'

'You won't get the bosses to worry about that sort of thing,' commented Moggy.

'You've got the point. Don't you see why there's got to be a union. They'll do it when we make them; not before.'

'Dad was right. You should have been a bleeding preacher.'

'You don't listen,' Keegan was almost shouting. 'None of you ever bloody well listen. You'll spend all your life fighting with your mates at the dock gates and never realize that if you would only get together and fight the bosses instead – '

'Who says I'm going to be a dockie all my life?'

'Got other plans, have you?' asked Fred, half teasing.

'I might have. I don't know.'

There was a pause while the union man waited to hear more, but Moggy did not intend to get on to the subject of his boxing. In the end it was Moggy who changed the subject.

'Going back for second call?'

Fred Keegan spoke quietly as if someone might be listening to them. 'I'll give you a tip, lad. They'll be unloading a shipment of oranges down at the Albert. She came in on the night tide. I heard from a mate of mine that they're in a hurry to turn round.'

'They won't unload oranges in the rain.'

'It'll stop by then,' replied Keegan hopefully. 'Walk over with me?'

'Yes. Thanks,' said Moggy. Then he added brutally, 'But I won't stand too close when we get there.'

Keegan proved correct on two counts. The rain had stopped by second call and there was indeed a ship-load of oranges to be unloaded at the Albert Docks. His informant, however, must have passed the word to a good many others as well as him, for, when they reached the docks, there were enough dockers waiting to eat the oranges, the ship, and the warehouse for good measure.

Moggy hung around on the edge of the crowd until he realized that he had no hope of getting taken on. The day was still damp and heavy and his sodden clothes clung uncomfortably to his body. Most of the men would be back again for third call; he could see them whispering in little knots, discussing with their closest mates where they were most likely to be taken on. But Moggy had had a bellyful for one day.

'Going home?' asked Fred Keegan, rejoining him again.

'Not much else to do.'

'I used to throw my hook in through the door to warn the missus I was back.'

'Used to?' asked Moggy.

'She started throwing it back at me. Now I use my cap. Safer.'

Moggy thought of all the times that he had seen his father sitting at home when he got back from school. He had no illusions about the welcome he would get.

73

'If you've nothing to do this evening come along to the meeting.'

'What meeting?'

'Union. We've got a good speaker.'

'You don't give up easy, do you?'

Fred looked at him and gave a little laugh. 'It's the only way with a Harris. If I let you be you'll end up like your dad. It won't take so bloody long either.'

'When is it, then?' asked Moggy gruffly.

Fred Keegan looked at him sharply. 'Thinking of coming, are you?'

'I just asked what time it was. What's wrong in that?' Moggy had not got any serious plans for going, but, with the water trickling down his neck, there seemed something to be said for hearing what the union lot had got to say.

'Seven o'clock. You know the hall. Just off the High Street.'

'Yes. I know.'

'See you, then?'

'I wouldn't lay odds on it, if I was you.'

Fred Keegan obviously decided that further pressure was pointless. 'You'd better be getting home,' he advised. 'Put on some dry clothes.'

'See you,' said Moggy. Then he added pointedly, 'See you sometime.'

Keegan looked up into the sky: 'Going to be a fine day. A lot of good that'll do us.' He pulled his cap down on his forehead, nodded at Moggy and walked off slowly.

More than on any other day Moggy would have liked to have taken a tram home, but he had not earned a penny and had only a few coppers left in his pocket. He meant to save those to give to Bob Tranter. One day, he thought, he might go to a union meeting – just to see what it was all about. But he had no intention of missing out on his training that evening.

Moggy was surprised to discover that his father was already sitting at the table in the front room by the time that he got home. Mrs Harris was working in the scullery, thumping and banging as she moved to express her displeasure.

'You was laid off quick, Dad,' said Moggy.

'Three hours. That's all we got. Three flaming hours.'

'Lucky to get that. Second call was worse than first. Must have been a thousand blokes left on the stones.'

Mrs Harris appeared in the doorway of the scullery, her hands dripping water. 'You too?'

'Didn't get work.'

'Fat lot of use you are,' she snapped.

'Lay off him,' snapped her husband. 'He's tried, ain't he?'

'I suppose he's brought back some money to feed your perishing kids.' She walked forward and held out a wet hand under Moggy's nose.

'I told you, I didn't work.'

'And I'm supposed to tell that to the kids, am I?'

'I gave you a tanner, didn't I?' shouted Mr Harris.

His wife rounded on him. 'Look, my man. I don't know how much you get paid but I know it's a fat lot more than that.' She reached forward to feel in her husband's pocket, but he smacked her hand away.

'You take what you're given, woman.'

'I can smell it,' she yelled. 'On your breath. How many pints did you sink on your way home?'

'Mind your own bleeding business.'

'That's the way, is it? Two bob for you. Sixpence for all the rest of us. Watch out we don't overeat.'

Moggy backed away from the row and walked quietly towards the scullery. His mother stopped him just before he reached the door.

'Don't you go in there, my boy.'

'I want to change, don't I? I'm wet.'

'Your clothes are in the wash.'

'That's bloody stupid,' protested Moggy, pitching in on his own account. 'Any fool could see we'd come back wet.'

'Don't you come it with me, you cheeky devil.' She took a swipe at Moggy's backside but he drew out of range without difficulty.

'We're both wet,' put in his father.

'You'll have to stay that way. You won't melt. Here.' She nodded to Moggy to come across to her. He hesitated. 'Let's feel you, then,' she said.

Reluctantly he crossed the room. Mrs Harris wiped her hands on her skirt and felt him round the shoulders. 'You're drying out well enough,' she announced. As if to reassure herself she passed her hand down the side of his leg.

Moggy did not react quickly enough when his mother felt the money in his pocket. Before he could get away she had pulled it out, turning the pocket inside out as she did so. She held the coppers tightly in her fist.

'You said you hadn't got no money,' she exclaimed.

'I never!' he protested. 'I said I didn't get no work. I saved that from yesterday.'

'Going to waste it like your father.'

'I want it,' shouted Moggy. He turned to his father. 'Tell her it's mine.'

Mr Harris seemed to have had enough of the row. 'Does it matter?' he asked.

'It would matter enough if it was your bloody money.'

Mrs Harris had edged over to the stairs, counting the coppers as she went. 'Five pence,' she said. 'That's eleven pence altogether. Do you two want this family to eat or don't you? Think I can feed them on air?'

Moggy was about to go after her but his father held him back. 'Keep your hair on,' he said.

'She ain't got no right to lift my money.'

'Here.' Mr Harris waited until his wife had lumbered up the stairs and then slipped twopence into his son's hand. 'A couple of mouldies for you, kid. And a lesson. Keep your paws in your pocket when the women are around. You've got to learn some day.'

'I was saving that money.'

'I'll take that back and all if you don't want it.'

Moggy kept a firm grip on the coppers his father had

given him and walked towards the scullery. Twopence was better than nothing, but he could hardly offer them to Bob Tranter for a lesson. He thought that Bob would probably be pleased enough to give him a work-out for nothing but, since he had always paid before, he did not like to ask. The scullery was full of steam from the copper in the corner. He had forgotten that it was washing day. Had he remembered he might have had more sense than to come home at all. Sure enough his change of clothes was lying in a sodden heap on the floor. He thought of washing himself over in some of the hot water from the copper but he could not bear the thought of taking off his wet clothes and then putting them on again.

'Is there anything to eat in this house?' he asked.

'Later on, when she cools down.'

'I ain't waiting,' he announced.

'Going back for third call?' asked his father.

'Like hell I am.'

'I thought I might try. There's plenty of time.'

'Well you can climb on some other geezer's back. I've stood about long enough for one day.'

'You'll stand about a lot more before you die. Get used to that idea.'

'It's a great shame, ain't it,' said Moggy sarcastically. He was definitely beginning to see what Fred Keegan had been on about. 'Give my love to the foreman. Hope he won't miss me too much.'

'Where are you going?'

'Knock about a bit. I won't go far on twopence, will I?'

Moggy slammed the door behind him as he walked into the street. The sun had come out and the day was rapidly turning hot. The rain was condensing into a steam which rose off the pavements and the roofs of the houses. Once outside Moggy had no idea what to do with himself. He had only had a bit of bread all day and he would hardly overeat on the couple of coppers in his pocket.

'Mog.' Doris called to him from the doorway of a

neighbour's house. She was sitting on the step with a friend about her own age.

He walked over and spoke to her brusquely. 'What do you want?'

'Give us a penny, Mog.'

'Drop dead.'

Doris's friend got up from the step and started to burrow into Moggy's pocket – fortunately the wrong one. 'Bloody women!' he shouted. 'You're all alike. Get out of there. I ain't giving you no money. I'm skint.'

'Mum still mad?'

'Go home and find out.'

'Ain't Dad's fault if they lays him off. Didn't you get no work neither?'

'Does it look like it?'

'I'm hungry,' whined Doris. 'Ain't you got a copper?'

'Go home and ask Mum. She took my money.'

'I don't want to go home.'

'Then you'll have to stay hungry, won't you?'

Moggy turned to go but Doris hung on to him. 'What are you going to do, Mog?' she asked.

Moggy shrugged; then an idea came to him on the spur of the moment. 'Go round and see Clara.'

'She your girl friend?'

'Not so's she'd notice.'

'Still at school, ain't she?'

'What's so wrong with that?' demanded Moggy aggressively.

'Don't let them out till four,' announced his sister.

'That's all you know,' retorted Moggy lamely. Then he added, 'Still dinner-time, ain't it?'

Moggy felt better the moment he had discovered a purpose in life. By the clock in a shop window it was nearly half past one. He did not know the time of afternoon school at Monza Street, but with a bit of luck, if he hurried, he had time to catch Clara before she went in.

He ran most of the way, fortifying himself with a

halfpenny bun as he went. When still some way from the school building he could tell that the children were outside by the noise they were making.

The playground was surrounded by a tall wire fence and a burly teacher stood on duty at the only gate. Moggy walked round the outside of the playground until at last he spotted Vicky and Clara, standing on their own, looking at the younger children playing with bored expressions on their faces.

Moggy caught the attention of a child and pointed towards them. 'Call those girls for me, will you?'

'What'll you give me?' asked the urchin promptly.

'For a favour,' replied Moggy. 'Go on.'

The child thought for a moment and then turned away to rejoin his friends. Moggy had to ask three times before he found a messenger who would do what he asked for nothing. When at last they got his message Vicky and Clara looked sharply over towards him. As soon as she spotted him Clara giggled and turned as if to walk in the other direction but Vicky hauled her back and together they walked over to the place where Moggy was hanging on to the wire.

'Where's your china?' asked Vicky at once.

'Jan? Ain't clapped eyes on him since that night we went to the Paragon. You see him often?'

Vicky tossed her head. 'None of your business.'

Clara winked at Moggy and shook her head behind her friend's back. 'I'll tell him you're pining if I see him,' said Moggy.

'Don't you dare,' replied Vicky. 'Anyway, there's more fish in the sea –'

'Perhaps he's shy,' broke in Moggy. 'Wants to know you care.'

'Don't tease her,' said Clara.

'What are you doing this afternoon?' Moggy asked Clara.

'What do you think I'm doing, half wit!'

'Can't you hop the wag?'

Clara looked over at the master on duty at the gate. 'Do you want me to climb out?'

'She don't play truant,' taunted Vicky. 'Clara's a good girl. I should have thought you'd found that out by this time.'

'Shut up, Vicky,' snapped Clara. She stood thoughtfully for a moment. 'I've got to register. I'll try and get out after that.' She turned to Vicky. 'We've got Sleepy Morgan all afternoon. He won't notice.'

'You going to do it?' asked Vicky in faint disbelief.

'Wait for me round the corner. Give me half an hour.'

The teacher on playground duty had left his position on the gate and was walking purposefully towards them.

'Beat it, now,' said Vicky. 'We ain't allowed to talk to people outside.'

'Don't know why they don't just lock you up and have done with it,' said Moggy.

As the teacher came near, the two girls became engrossed in an interesting conversation and turned away as if they had no interest in him. Moggy's first instinct was to turn and run, but he reminded himself that teachers had nothing on him any longer so he stood his ground and looked him in the eye.

'What are you hanging around here for?' asked the man.

'It's a free country, ain't it?' replied Moggy.

'Shouldn't you be at school?'

'I ain't a school kid,' replied Moggy. 'I work, don't I?'

'Shouldn't you be at work, then?'

Moggy stared in the teacher's face. 'That's my business, ain't it?'

The teacher seemed ready to become angry. 'Get away from here,' he ordered. 'You're not allowed to talk to our pupils.'

Moggy drew breath to answer him back, but thought better of it. Very slowly he stepped back a few paces from the wire. The teacher watched him carefully until he reckoned that he had retreated far enough. Then he turned and continued his tour of the playground.

Moggy watched the kids playing until the bell rang and the burly teacher organized them all into silent lines, ready to march back into the school. Then he ambled off to wait for Clara out of sight of the building.

'I came as soon as I could.' Clara was panting as she ran round the corner. She stood awkwardly, smiling at Moggy, yet keeping her distance.

'Glad you made it.'

'Not working?' asked Clara.

'On the stones,' replied Moggy. 'It's the rain that does it.'

'What are we going to do?'

'Feel like going up to town?'

'Got anything to spend?'

Moggy took the penny-halfpenny out of his pocket and held it towards her. 'I'm skint,' he said.

'What's the use of that?'

'It ain't far to walk.'

'I ain't walking,' she protested. 'Who do you think I am?'

'Let's go down the Garden, then,' he suggested.

'I don't know,' she replied uncertainly. 'The kids say the school board man knocks around there to pick up truants.'

Moggy could see that she had begun to regret coming out. 'You been caught before?' he asked. She shook her head. 'What are you fussing for? They only give you a load of jaw first time. I know.'

He grabbed her hand and led her in the direction of the Spitalfields Garden. At first he had to encourage her along, but soon her spirits revived and she walked alongside him. After a time she relaxed enough to put her hand on his arm.

'Oh, you're all wet,' she exclaimed.

'It rained this morning. Perhaps you weren't awake early enough to see.'

'Of course I saw,' replied Clara. 'You'll catch your death, going about like that.'

'The sun's out, ain't it?' said Moggy.

On the way they called in at a shop to invest one third of Moggy's capital on a small bag of aniseed balls, which they sucked as they walked.

Spitalfields Garden was looking rather better than usual. The rain had washed away the dirt and litter and the grass, which was usually a dull brown colour, was distinctly green. A group of girls were bowling a hoop along the main path, which was lined with park benches. Moggy and Clara tried to find somewhere to sit, but every bench was already occupied by a sleeping figure, each huddled in rags and newspaper.

'It's all right for some,' said Moggy. 'Sleep all night and sleep all day. Want to take the weight off your feet?'

'Wouldn't mind,' replied Clara.

'I'll get you a seat, then.' He looked round until he saw a shape which looked suitably old and female. Tip-toeing over, he bent down until his head was right by the newspaper which covered the face. Then he cupped his hands, drew in a deep breath and let out a full-throated shout. The old woman gave a little yelp and sat up abruptly. Immediately Moggy sat down on the section of the seat vacated by her head, and pulled Clara down on top of him.

The woman looked bewildered for a few moments while she gathered her senses; then she began calling them names.

'It's Lushy Sue,' said Moggy.

'Who's she?' asked Clara.

'An old soak.' Then he shouted back in the old woman's face. 'Getting a bit of shut-eye before the boozer opens are you?' He made a face and started to chant Bet's song:

> 'Lushy Sue, Lushy Sue,
> Look what gin has done to you.'

The old woman spat like a snake and started to claw at them both. Clara jumped up and let out a shriek.

'She's alive,' she cried.

'Only just,' laughed Moggy, fending off Lushy Sue's hands.

'No, I mean her hair. Look.'

Moggy had seen enough lice – from time to time his mother found a few on his own scalp – but he had never seen a whole head of hair move before his eyes. He felt the vomit rise in his throat.

'Leave her be,' pleaded Clara. 'I couldn't sit on that seat. Not after her.'

A lump of saliva narrowly missed Moggy's arm as he rose from the seat to join Clara. Lushy Sue was now launched into a volley of swearing. The individual words had no meaning, but the voice raked on and on at them, like a circular saw cutting its way through wood.

'Belt up, you old bag,' shouted Moggy. As he stared into her eyes he felt a moment of panic. The kids said she was a witch; as she rose up after him, her face twisted with anger, she certainly looked capable of working evil.

Clara turned and ran off. Moggy did not like to give way before an old woman, but, once Clara had gone, he had an excuse to follow her. The swearing stopped as abruptly as it had begun. As soon as Lushy Sue realized that she had driven off the intruders she settled back on to her bench and drew her rags around her. She did not, however, put the paper back over her face but watched through narrow eyes as Moggy caught up with Clara and the two of them dropped on to their knees at the other side of the shabby garden.

'Bet says she was crossed in love,' announced Moggy at last. He tried to keep his voice as light as possible to show that the old woman's anger had had no effect on him.

'Who'd love her?' asked Clara with a shudder.

'You don't know what she was like, do you?'

Clara picked a piece of grass and put in in her mouth. Then she stared over his shoulder at the sky.

'Penny for them,' said Moggy at last.

Clara knelt upright and stuck out her palm. 'Go on, then. Give it me.'

'What?'

'A penny. I shan't tell you what I was thinking unless you do.'

Moggy took his last penny out of his pocket and held it in front of her face. 'There you are then.'

Clara did not take it. 'Is your mum good looking?' she asked at last.

'Good looking!' Moggy laughed out loud. 'She's got a phiz like the back of a bleeding bus.'

'Nice and slim, is she?'

'Here, what are you getting at?' demanded Moggy suspiciously.

'You wanted to know what I was thinking about,' replied Clara.

'Don't tell me you were thinking about my mum.'

Clara stared across the garden. 'Do you ever feel as though someone's walked over your grave?' she asked at last.

'You're barmy,' announced Moggy.

'No really –' She was leaning forward now and looking at him with anxious eyes. 'That's what I felt when she was yelling at us.'

'What's it got to do with our mum?'

'What would you feel like if you was your dad, going to sleep beside her? Look!' She gripped Moggy's wrist as she talked. 'I bet there was a time when your dad looked forward to getting into bed with your mum. You know, when she was young and pretty.'

Moggy tried to make the mental adjustment, but his mind baulked at the attempt.

'Would you feel like that with me?'

'What do you mean?' Moggy stammered a bit, feeling that the conversation was getting out of hand.

'You know bleeding well what I mean or you're greener than you're cabbage looking.' Moggy was lost for an answer, but Clara spared him the trouble. 'I ain't offering, so you can get that out of your murky little head.' She looked at him for a moment and then shook her head, as if despairing of making him understand.

'I walked up to the West End with Vicky last week,' said Clara at last. 'We stood and watched the people coming out of the theatre. There was women there – thin and beautiful they was. Must have been all of fifty. How old's your mum?'

'I don't know.' He did a sum in his head. 'About thirty-five.'

'Will I be fat and ugly when I'm thirty-five?' Clara looked over at the seat where Lushy Sue was just settling down to sleep again. 'How do you know I won't end up like that?' She ran her hands through her hair as if to make sure that there were no lice there.

'Leave off,' protested Moggy. 'She's drinking herself to death. You wouldn't do that.'

Clara spun round on him. 'How do you know I wouldn't? If you married me, how could you be sure I wouldn't end up like that? What's your mother's life but bloody babies, bloody scrubbing, bloody – '

'For Christ's sake don't get steamed up. I ain't going to marry you.'

'Very sure about it,' she said pertly.

'Look, you don't have to get married at all.'

'No,' she mused. 'I think I'll find work in Piccadilly and catch the virgin's bus back on Saturday night. There's good money in it.'

'What are you going on like this for?'

'You wanted to know what I was thinking about. Here!' She opened up her hand. 'I ain't had my penny.'

Moggy held the coin up in front of her face. 'Take it.'

'Don't be daft,' she said, pushing it away. 'I'm only joking.'

'Like hell you've been joking.'

Clara leant forward on to the damp grass and began to pull the heads off daisies. 'That old bag walked over my grave all right,' she said. 'Sent shivers down my spine. I do sometimes wonder what it's like to be old. When nobody wants you. It's all right for them ladies that don't

85

have to slave their guts out and get Sweet Fanny Adams for it.'

'You sound like the preacher.'

'I didn't know you went to church.'

'It's what we call Fred Keegan, the union man. He was rabbiting on this morning.'

'I'd join the union if I was a bloke,' announced Clara sharply. 'I think I'll start a union for women like your mum.'

'You sound like one of them suffragettes.'

'Why not?' she asked. 'I reckon they had the right idea.'

'You'd better go to the union meeting tonight then. Find out how to do it,' teased Moggy.

'You going?'

'No. Got to get some training in.' He made a few passes at the air. 'I'm fighting again Sunday. Feel like coming?'

Clara had got over her outburst. She looked at him in a tantalizing way and pursed her lips. 'I don't know what I'm doing yet, do I?'

'Don't force yourself,' retorted Moggy. He was beginning to become irritated with her but he covered it up well enough.

She looked at him and cocked her head on one side. 'I think I'll come,' she declared. 'I could get a taste for boxing.' She put a hand up to his face. 'Your nose bleeds easy, don't it?'

'I told you. I've got a weakness. Bob Tranter says it ain't nothing to worry about. Not like cutting round the eyes.'

'I ain't worrying,' Clara assured him. 'Me, I like the sight of blood.'

'But you don't like nits, do you?' He was pleased to have found a chink in her defensive system. He bent over as if to examine her head. 'Bet your hair's all crawling with them.'

'It ain't,' she snapped. She jumped to her feet and shook out her hair. 'I'm fed up with this place. That copper's burning a hole in your pocket. Let's go and spend it.'

'Didn't they give you no dinner at school?'

'Ugh!' She pulled a face. 'Call that dinner?'

Moggy thought that it was probably better than a bit of bread and a bun, but he let it pass. 'We won't do much on this.'

'Don't matter,' she said. She smiled at him; then she looked round at the sleeping figures on the benches. 'Bleeding graveyard gets on your nerves. Let's get out of here.'

5

While the bad times continued, Clara and Vicky got into the habit of keeping a look-out for Moggy during the dinner hour, and sure enough, more often than not, he would show up and hang on the railings to talk to them for as long as the teacher on duty would permit. Clara admitted that Sleepy Morgan had not noticed her absence on the first afternoon, but nothing would convince her to try it on again. Moggy could therefore only kick around the streets, waiting for her to come out at the end of afternoon school. Even then, however, there was never much to do without money, but at least Clara's company filled up the hours before Bob Tranter would be home, fed and rested, ready to give his pupil his evening work-out.

Moggy sometimes felt bad about turning up for his lesson with nothing in his pocket. Deep down he felt that a professional arrangement was a professional arrangement. But Bob would not hear of him cutting training just because he had no money to pay for it. He used to laugh and say that any manager had to be prepared to sink a bit in a long term investment, and one day Moggy would repay him handsomely. At least it was obvious that the ex-boxer enjoyed the time with his pupil. The evenings spent sparring in the back yard kept him in touch with a way of life that he had left behind him.

Moggy fought twice at Premierland in June, winning once and losing once. If anything the fight he lost did him the more good. Another boxer had fallen out at the last moment and Bob Tranter offered Moggy to fill the gap. He found himself up against a lad considerably older than himself in a spot well up the bill. The hall was more than half full, and from the noise it seemed that the crowd enjoyed the scrap. There was no doubt at the end as to which of the two had won, but the referee had called for a special round of applause for Moggy Harris — a lad with a great future. Bob Tranter had been the first to warn him against over-confidence: Moggy had to remember that he had lost, and it was better to be booed out of the ring after winning the verdict than to get himself a reputation as a plucky loser. Moggy did not need telling.

Slowly, as the weeks went by, he was beginning to add a little technique to his natural fighter's temperament. Sometimes Bob tried to convince him to keep a check on his instinctive aggression. One day, he warned, he would meet a boxer who knew how to keep out of the way of his two-fisted assaults. He had to learn to defend — even to retreat if need be. Since he was still Bob's only pupil, Moggy was short of sparring partners and in the course of time he learned how to counter many of the old professional's tricks. Just occasionally, however, Bob would unleash something approaching his full power. Moggy's head reeled under the rain of blows, but still he stood square to the assault, even shuffling forward in his flat-footed way, looking for the opening for his own counter-attack. In the end, however, Bob always drew back.

'Watch yourself!'

'What's wrong?'

'You dropped your guard.' The old pro's glove would land at half power on Moggy's chin. 'I could have put you down. Tweet tweet — curtains.'

'I didn't know.'

'You wouldn't know anything after I'd clobbered you, laddy. Guard up. Chin down. Box on.'

The two of them circled and bored in at each other as they moved round the tiny back yard, until in the end Bob Tranter would drop his gloves and call it a day. Sometimes the kids in Bet's crowd would watch the training, sitting like birds on the wall around the yard. At first Moggy had been embarrassed to box with them watching him, but, as his confidence increased, he grew to like having a gallery.

Occasionally Clara deigned to come and watch. He would have liked to have thought that she came out of devotion, but it was more that she found herself increasingly at a loose end. Vicky had run into Jan Jaworski again and they had taken up where they had left off on the night they went to the music hall. Jan had found a regular job, cleaning up at the bus depot. Although hardly well paid, at least it brought in steady money. He could therefore afford to take Vicky to the pictures and into cafés. As long as the docks were slack the best that Moggy could do for Clara was to buy her the occasional bun. It was hardly a diet on which to build a great romance, but then, Clara did not seem to be looking for a great romance. As time went on she became quite a useful critic of his developing style. But Bob and Clara never really got on together. He tolerated her sitting in the corner of the yard because she was a friend of Moggy's, but he made it quite clear that he preferred it when she left them on their own.

At least Moggy's boxing gave him an interest while things remained bad at the docks. By the end of June everyone in the East End seemed poor and dispirited. First affected, of course, were the dockers themselves and their families, but, as the weeks passed, others began to feel the pinch as well. Shop-keepers and market stall-holders had to display large notices, announcing: NO TICK GIVEN. Those who in normal times would have shopped early, when prices were at their proper level, now held back. Children stood around the markets in droves, waiting for the goods to be knocked down in price. The stall-holders, for their part, did all they could to fend off the evil moment so that they could sell the largest possible proportion of their wares at a profit. Most of the kids at North Road School forgot what it was like to set off in the morning with a good breakfast inside them. The teachers, desperate to keep the attention of their hungry charges, took to giving the children a slice of bread and treacle as they arrived. Some said that Mr Pender paid for the food out of his own pocket, but no one knew whether to believe the rumour or not. Moggy was inclined to be cynical. He had gone to school hungry often enough and nobody had given him anything to eat. It seemed unlikely to him that Mr Pender would suddenly have discovered a generous streak in himself.

To begin with, the Harris family did rather better than most. As an old hand, Moggy's dad had got the business of finding work down to a fine art.

For as long as he could remember Moggy had heard his mother complain at the way that her husband insisted on going out to the pub, night in, night out, even when there was barely enough money to provide everyone with a square meal. At the time it had seemed a reasonable enough complaint. It was not until Moggy became a docker himself that he came to recognize that it was all part of an established routine of finding work; over the years Curly Harris had learnt in which pubs he was most likely to meet up with the supervisors. Once inside, with a pint of beer in his hand, he would sidle round the bar until he had worked himself into a strategic position. Then, at a well judged moment, he would make his presence known.

'Mr Jackson. Remember me, Curly Harris? Did a good job for you on that jute last week. Is your glass empty, Mr Jackson? Feel like another?'

Next morning he would be shouting out at the dock gate. 'Mr Jackson. It's me, Curly Harris.' The message was clear enough: 'You got a pint off me last night, governor. Now it's your turn to do me a favour.'

Moggy had never much liked creeping. He could not see Fred Keegan buying the supervisors drinks at night. But then, when there was work going, Curly went inside while Fred was left on the stones. Of course, during an evening in the pub, his father also had quite a few pints on his own account. He also treated friends who had nothing to give him except the scraps of information which dockers passed from one to another every night.

The night's drinking never seemed to have too much

effect on Mr Harris. In the morning he was always one of the earliest out of his bed. In normal times it was usually good enough to be at the dock gate half to three-quarters of an hour before the supervisors were due to appear, but when bad times arrived a hard core of fanatics would compete with one another to secure places in the very front row.

Morning after morning Moggy found himself being booted out of bed at the most unearthly hour. His father would hardly let him dress before they set off towards the dock where, according to his information, they would be most likely to find work. Once installed by the chain in the very front row they sometimes had two or two and a half hours to put in, while the crowd filled up behind them.

Moggy sometimes suspected that his father actually enjoyed the competition to get work. It was as if he could prove something to himself by showing that he was just the kind of worker the employers needed – that he was the one man who would get work when everyone else was left on the stones. Sometimes, as he waited through the long morning hours, Moggy would begin to feel that he could see what Fred Keegan was on about. It really did not seem beyond the wit of man to devise some system of labour by which men would turn up for work at a reasonable hour in the morning, and know that there would be a job for them when they got there.

It was, after all, natural that Moggy should take a dim view of the system, because his short nights and early morning walks were nearly always so much wasted effort. By using every trick in the book Curly Harris was able to get a certain amount of work for himself, but there was very little that he could do to help his son. When labour was tight, nobody was prepared to take on a boy. In his heart Moggy knew that it was a waste of time for him even to try, but his father expected it of him, and it did not seem right to let him down.

However, by going out in the morning, at least he got

out of the house for a few hours. On the whole Moggy kept out as much as he could. The place seemed full of people and clashing temperaments. During June his mother had seemed suddenly to grow even more pregnant. Tired and anxious, she was ready to vent her frustration on anything that moved across her line of vision during the day. Bet was now rarely seen at North Road School, as she was kept at home to take care of the baby. The school board man called a couple of times, but even he seemed beaten by the general atmosphere of dockland and allowed himself to be fobbed off by any feeble excuse, concocted on the spur of the moment for his benefit.

Moggy had known many such periods and he assumed that they would survive it as they had survived the others. Disaster struck one Thursday morning at the beginning of July when Mr Harris simply failed to get out of bed. Other men skipped the odd day often enough, but all the children knew that with Mr Harris it was different. The moment they heard that he had stayed in bed they knew that he had cracked – that he had withdrawn from the competition – and that, until things got better, he would not stir out of the house.

Moggy expected his mother to follow suit and fold up under all the strains. Instead she rose to the occasion. If anything her temper became a little easier as she settled down to the hard business of keeping the family alive. Moggy managed to get the occasional morning's work, and he handed over all the money that he earned. It did not amount to very much, but somehow Mrs Harris managed to rake up at least one meal a day, even though it meant that she had to dig deep into the money stored away in her private hiding place. At last she announced that, since they could not go on as they were, they would have to let off the top floor of the house. Next day a notice went up in the front window advertising two rooms immediately available at a low rent. For a week nobody showed any interest and Moggy continued to hope that the bad times would end before anyone took up the offer.

One day, however, he returned from the dock gate to find the house in chaos. Fred Keegan, the union man, having been thrown out of his own house for failing to pay the rent, was moving his half-starved family into the two upstairs rooms. As Moggy came through the front door Keegan and his father were struggling on the stairs with the huge Harris matrimonial bed. Moggy stood and watched for some minutes until his father spotted him and let out a torrent of abuse at him for standing by, doing nothing. It seemed impossible that the bed could ever be negotiated round the corner at the bottom of the stairs. Mr Harris swore that at some time in the distant past it had been carried up the stairs, and what went up had to come down. After a great deal of heaving and swearing they managed to get it round the corner and into the room.

Mrs Harris supervised as they tried it, first in one place, then in another, but wherever they put it it dominated the living-room to such an extent that there was barely space left even for the tables and chairs.

'We'll have to get rid of it,' announced Mr Harris.

'I'll not sell it,' retorted his wife sharply. 'It's the only decent stick of furniture we've got.'

'Decent!' exclaimed Moggy. 'It's a load of scrap. Look, all the paint's peeling off.'

'Any old iron!' called out Bet, coming out of the corner where she had been skulking.

Mrs Harris lashed out in the direction of her daughter's head but missed by feet. 'You hold your trap, you cheeky monkey.'

'We could pawn it,' suggested Mr Harris.

'You'd have to pay 'em to take it,' said Moggy.

'I ain't going to let it go,' insisted Mrs Harris, almost sobbing. 'It's my bed.'

'Our bed,' corrected her husband.

'It came from my gran's house.'

'Don't owe you anything, then, does it?' put in Moggy.

'You hold your trap, and all,' snapped his mother.

'What do you think, Fred?' Mr Harris looked round for an impartial opinion, but Fred Keegan had wisely withdrawn to let the family settle its own problem.

'Where are the rest of us going to sleep?' asked Bet.

'We'll have you girls in here.'

'The table –' protested Bet.

'You can sleep under the bloody table, can't you?' shouted her mother.

'What about us?' put in Moggy.

'There's room for you and Charlie in the scullery. With the baby.'

'For Christ's sake!' exclaimed Moggy. 'We won't get our mattresses in there.'

'Then you can sleep on the bloody floor,' shouted his mother. 'If you don't like it you can blooming well lump it. Nobody's forcing you to stay. If your father could find some work –'

'Lay off dada, won't you?' yelled Bet. 'If there ain't no ships in –'

'Fat lot he'd know if a whole bleeding fleet came in during the night.'

Mr Harris did not defend himself but slumped wearily on to the offending bed. He was not allowed to remain there, however, as there were odds and ends still to be moved down from upstairs. Fred Keegan's possessions then had to be brought round in a barrow and carried upstairs. By the time that the whole operation was completed the little house was crammed full of people and furniture. The noise of the Keegan family settling in upstairs got on Mrs Harris's nerves and before long everybody was snapping at one another. To make matters worse the stove went out and the evening meal was delayed. Moggy was starving, but he had had enough of the family and could not face hanging around any longer.

'I'm off,' he announced.

'Don't you want no grub?' asked Bet surprised.

'Not in this loony-bin.'

'Got some splosh to buy some, then?' she asked.

95

'I'm skint,' he confessed. Then he added, 'I'll find something.'

'Watch it, Mog,' she pleaded, suddenly concerned. 'Don't get pinched.'

'Why should I get pinched?' demanded Moggy crossly.

'You won't find nothing lying about in the streets, that's for sure.'

'I can look after myself, can't I?' he retorted.

Moggy saw Bet look at him with big, worried eyes as he turned away from her. It was easy enough for him to snap her head off, but she had hit on the problem right enough. In bad times the kids swept the streets clean of anything fit – or even almost fit – to eat. If an apple fell off a stall in the market there were half a dozen hands ready to grab at it. There were altogether too many people with itchy fingers round dockland when work was bad, and so shop-keepers and market traders kept one beady eye trained on their wares.

In the end it came down to a simple choice. Moggy could either stay out and go to bed hungry, or he could go back again at about the time that the meal would be ready and trust to luck that Bet did not hold it over him. Usually he would have gone without food, but after some consideration he decided that he really was too hungry to see it through. As far as possible, however, from then onwards, Moggy used the house only as a place to eat and sleep and both Clara and Bob Tranter saw a good deal more of him, than did members of the Harris family. Not that anyone really missed him! There were far too many people in the house and one less eased the strain on everyone else.

The arrangement would have been just about tolerable to Moggy if only he had been able to get a decent night's sleep. Since the scullery floor was really not big enough for Charlie and the baby as well as him, Moggy had to wedge himself in between the legs of the cot and the big copper.

After a couple of weeks even Clara – who generally was treated to the better side of Moggy's nature – noticed that he was getting very short-tempered. It was partly lack of sleep, but the way they lived was getting on everybody's nerves.

Within a matter of days the relationship between the two families in the house had grown very strained. Mistakenly the Harrises had made no conditions about the number of visitors that the Keegans could receive, and night after night stern-eyed union men picked their way across the floor of the front room, dodging between the bed and the table, on their way to the stairs.

'Always bloody well holding meetings,' grumbled Mr Harris. 'Don't know why they don't put a plaque on the door – "Union Headquarters".'

'Don't know why we don't charge them more rent for it,' said his wife. Then she paused. 'That's not such a bad idea either. You tell him – '

There were a hundred things that Mr Harris had to tell his lodger, but none of the messages ever got delivered. Somehow Fred Keegan managed to fend them off by being completely oblivious of the bad feeling his activities were stirring up downstairs. He had other things on his mind. Sometimes, when the house was quiet, Moggy could hear the men's voices upstairs, talking, talking, talking. They seemed to be planning something, almost as if it were a military operation and, as the days passed, they seemed to grow ever more excited and expectant.

Mrs Harris railed at her husband for failing to bring the tenants into line. She would have done it herself, but her own relationships with the Keegans had gone beyond the limit of rational discussion. She was, for one thing, waging a private war over the use of her territory as a right of way to the toilet in the backyard. Mr Harris begged her to be reasonable; when nature called, the Keegan family had no option but to go out through the scullery. His wife accepted this in principle, but she insisted that no bladders on earth could need emptying as often as those belonging to the three Keegan girls. The rest of the family usually managed to restrain her from hurling abuse at them as they walked through the scullery door but Mrs Harris would not budge from her conviction; either they were given a damned sight more to drink than was good for them, or the whole thing was a plot, specially devised to annoy her.

In the first week of August it looked as if employment in the port had taken a turn for the better. As a boy, Moggy still found it hard to get taken on, but the older dockers began to get three, or sometimes even four days' work a week. Goaded by his wife, Curly Harris at last managed to snap back into gear and get out to work in the morning. With money at last coming into the house again, Mrs Harris began to lay plans for evicting her unwelcome tenants.

It was just then that the tally clerks chose to go on strike. With nobody to check goods in and out of the warehouses, activity on the river ground to a halt once again. Mrs Harris laid the blame squarely at Fred Keegan's door. Moggy and his father vainly tried to convince her that the tally clerks had a separate union and Keegan, as a dockie's man, could hardly be blamed for what they did. But Mrs Harris would not hear of such subtleties. If there were no unions, she declared, then there would be no strikes; an honest man would be able to do an honest day's work. Moggy thought that his mother sounded as bad as Mr Pender on the last day of term, but he had long since learnt that nothing was gained by trying to make her change her mind once it was made up.

The balloon went up on a Sunday dinner-time when Mrs Harris decided to tell Fred Keegan just what she thought about his union activities. She grabbed hold of him as he slid as unobtrusively as possible past the table where the Harris family was eating.

'Here, Keegan.' She dragged him back towards her.

'Yes?' Fred looked down at her uncertainly.

'What're we supposed to eat?' she demanded aggressively.

Keegan looked so puzzled that Moggy tried to come to

his aid. 'It ain't nothing to do with him. We've told you.'

'Shut your face, young man,' snapped his mother. 'You, Keegan. I asked you what we was supposed to eat.'

Fred Keegan tried to peer into the dish which was in front of Mr Harris. 'I don't understand.'

'It's your mates are out on strike, ain't it? Things was just getting better. Now you've started it all again.'

'I told you, it ain't his union,' protested her husband.

Moggy watched Fred Keegan's face as he began to understand what she was going on about. He thought that he had never seen anybody change so quickly. One moment Keegan was friendly and his voice was quiet; the next he had gone red in the face and his voice was loud and angry.

'Don't you blame the bloody unions, missus,' he shouted. 'If you've got something to say, tell the bosses. See what they say.'

Mrs Harris heaved herself to her feet and snatched some papers out of Keegan's hand. 'What've you got here?' she demanded. 'Are they all about the strike? How you planned it?'

In one movement Mrs Harris hurled the papers through the open front door. Moggy could see the union man's blood pressure rise a point or two, but he did not let the loss of his papers deter him from his line of argument.

'Christ, missus!' declared Fred. 'Your family's been half starved for two bleeding months. Why? Because the bosses wouldn't give Curly any work, that's why.' He looked across the table and caught Moggy's eye. 'How many days' work has the kid done since he started?'

'As many as you, that's for sure,' shouted Mrs Harris. 'He's got to get a good name before they'll take him on regular, like Curly.'

'Teaching him to lick the bosses' arse, are you?' sneered Keegan. 'Got the taste yet, kid?'

Mrs Harris's voice rose to a high pitch. 'Don't you be vulgar in my house. And I won't have you leading our Mog astray. He's got a living to earn.'

Keegan paused for a moment and the anger drained out

of his face as quickly as it had come. His eyes stared into Moggy's before he spoke. 'Moggy don't need telling. He knows.'

Mrs Harris rounded on Moggy. 'What've you been telling him?' she demanded.

'I ain't told him nothing,' protested Moggy.

'He don't have to tell me,' said Keegan. 'That one's not going to be content with this bloody life.' He waved his hand round the room. 'It stands out a mile.'

'He's going to be a puggy,' put in Bet.

'Don't talk rubbish,' retorted her mother.

'Straight up,' insisted Bet. 'He's good enough to be a proper pro.'

Keegan looked across the table, but Moggy avoided his eye. 'You don't have to get out of the docks, Mog. We've got to make them better.'

'How're you going to do that?' asked Mr Harris wearily.

'I reckon we've got to have a strike.'

Mrs Harris banged her fist on the table. 'You've got one, ain't you? What more do you want?'

'We're just playing at it, that's the trouble. We won't get anything done till we bring the whole bleeding country to a standstill. Docks, pits, roads, railways. The lot. Nothing happens till you make it happen.'

'You're off your perishing rocker,' shouted Mrs Harris. 'What good would you do? You tell me that.'

'We'd have a revolution.'

There was a pause while the announcement sank in. Then Mrs Harris found her voice. 'Here! You ain't planning no revolution. Not in my house. Get him out, Curly, before they start fighting.'

'Like Russia?' asked Moggy.

'Not that sort of revolution.' The union man looked around the cramped living-room. 'Christ, how do I make you understand? That's what it's all about – making tens of thousands of bloody Harrises understand.' He turned on Moggy. 'Haven't you seen enough, kid? Do you want to

100

go on fighting with your mates at the dock gates all your life?'

Moggy looked for an answer, but his mother saved him the trouble. 'It's been good enough for his dad.'

'If that's the most you want for your children, why the hell do you bother to have another.' Keegan pointed at her bulging stomach.

She nodded towards her husband. 'Blame him for – '

Mr Harris interrupted her routine justification. 'Takes two, don't it?'

'Stop going on at one another and think of the baby,' snapped Keegan. 'Is this all you want for your kids?'

'What'd your lot do about it, then?' asked Moggy aggressively.

'Look! We paralyse the country. Bring everything to a stop see?'

'Then?' Mrs Harris was looking at him with withering scorn.

'Then, we take over.'

'Take over – what?'

'Factories, docks. The lot.'

'Who's we?'

'The workers. Curly for one. And Moggy.'

Mrs Harris looked at her menfolk in disbelief. 'Them two going to run the docks?' Her shriek of laughter made Moggy bridle.

'How can I make you believe in yourselves?'

'Right pig's ear you lot'd make of running the docks,' said Mrs Harris.

'They're not so bloody wonderful now, are they? One thing; we'd use labour properly. Not take a man today and discard him tomorrow.'

'Be loading flour in the banana boat more likely. A few weeks of that and there wouldn't be a single bleeding ship on the Thames. You'd be on the stones; the whole lot of you.'

'We've got men who could do it.'

'Some of you can write, can you?' sneered Mrs Harris.

'Ernie Bevin's better than any of the bosses.'

'Ah – go on!'

Fred Keegan turned on Moggy for support. 'Tell her, kid. Tell her what it's like. We've got to change it.'

The room went quiet as Moggy thought about his answer. It suddenly mattered what he said. Keegan wanted his backing; his mother was looking to him to maintain family solidarity against the hated intruder.

'You're dead right in most of it, Fred. It's all wrong, the way they treat us dockies.'

'There you are,' declared the union man triumphantly.

Moggy brought him down to earth sharply. 'You're off your perishing rocker, all the same.'

'Why? What's wrong with what I've said.'

'The docks is lolly, ain't they? Lots of lovely lolly. You don't think the bosses're going to hand it all over, just because we go on strike.'

'We've got to be united.'

'Look, matey,' said Moggy. 'If you was a short-arse like me, you'd have learnt the first lesson. If you wants something bad you've got to fight for it.'

Fred Keegan seemed taken aback. 'It doesn't have to be violent.'

'No?' declared Moggy. 'You just wait and see who starts getting violent when you puts picket lines across the dock gates and nobody can't get nothing to eat. Remember, the bosses have got the fuzz. And the army.'

'They're working men too,' protested Keegan.

'Working men, my Aunt Fanny. Just wait and see which side they fight on, matey.'

By disagreeing with both his parents and Fred Keegan, Moggy had taken the steam out of the row. Mrs Harris glowered down at her plate, while her husband attempted to restore relationships.

'I know you don't mean no harm, Fred,' he said.

'Do you want us to leave?' asked the union man.

'Yes I do,' put in Mrs Harris. 'He put those ideas into the boy's head.'

'We need the money,' snapped her husband.

'Got us by the short and curlies, ain't he. Stops my men working so's we can't kick him out.'

'We'll go if you want, Mrs Harris. A couple of days – '

She bit her lip. 'Stay if you've got to. Just keep out from under my feet.'

Keegan looked at Mr Harris for confirmation, and he nodded.

'Just remember, Fred, this ain't no union headquarters.'

The two men exchanged a glance before Fred turned to walk up the stairs. Mrs Harris waited till he had almost reached the top before pushing her head up the stairs after him.

'And tell those girls of yours not to drink so bleeding much.'

Keegan turned at the top of the stairs. 'Drink? What do you mean? They're only kids.'

'Water's as bad as gin,' shouted Mrs Harris. 'Twice a day. That's all they need. You'd think this room was Piccadilly Circus.' Keegan slammed the door upstairs, leaving her to vent her frustration on her husband and son. She looked from one to the other, and then burst out crying. 'Fine bloody men you are. You'd think I'd get some support from my own flesh and blood.' She turned on her husband. 'I saw the look you gave him. Don't pay any attention to her. Just making a fuss, am I? You heard him! Revolution indeed!'

'There'll be a revolution in this bleeding house if you don't dry up,' retorted her husband.

'It's all right for you. You don't live here all day. I'm the one who has to put up with them.'

'They ain't too bad, Mum,' said Bet.

'Nobody asked you to speak, my girl.' Her mother's voice rose to shrill pitch.

Upstairs the Keegans were moving about and the girls

started to shout at one another. Mrs Harris tried to shut the noise out of her head, but it seemed as though the lodgers were specially intent on goading her.

'You go up,' she said to her husband. 'Tell them there are other people in this house.'

'They're all right,' grumbled Curly.

'Tell them,' shouted his wife. 'Why should I do it?'

'Don't do it then. Leave them be.'

Suddenly Moggy could stand it no longer. The house was too small for so many people. He could not bear the thought of sleeping on the scullery floor with Charlie and the baby or being cramped in the four square yards of the main room which was not taken up with the huge bed.

'I'm going out,' he said quietly. Neither of his parents took any notice, so he repeated his statement: 'I'm going out. Don't expect me back.'

'Get lost, then,' snapped his mother.

Mr Harris looked down at his hands and kept his mouth tight shut.

'Keep an eye open for me at the dock gate, Dad.'

His father looked up. There was no surprise in his eyes; he had obviously been expecting Moggy to go sometime. 'Think I'll go to St Katherine's tomorrow,' he said. 'They're all as bad as each other.'

Moggy lifted his coat and a couple of sacks. 'See you, then. I'll look back soon.'

Mrs Harris looked at him in silence. Then, just as he was about to leave, she called quietly, 'If you're hungry, Mog . . .'

'There's too many of us in this house.' He looked up at the ceiling. 'I'll come back when they've gone.'

'But if you're hungry –'

'Don't worry. I ain't going far. I'll look in.'

'Got any money?' asked his father. When Moggy shook his head he took sixpence out of his pocket. 'A tanner. It's all I've got, lad.'

Moggy took it and nodded. Then he put on his cap and walked out. Fred Keegan's papers lay in the street where they had landed.

'Fred.' Moggy called up to the window above his head. After he had called a second time the window opened and Keegan's head appeared. Moggy stirred the papers with his foot. 'Here. The plans for the revolution. You'd better pick them up before the coppers come and read them.'

Keegan nodded and disappeared into the room but Moggy did not wait to help him. Slinging his sacks over his shoulder he set off at a brisk walk towards Cable Street.

6

Moggy spent the rest of the day as if nothing had happened. He was at his place by the gate when Clara and Vicky came out of school and they picked Jan up an hour or so later. He had managed to get through most of his wages and had only a shilling in his pocket. Moggy had sixpence. It was all he had for food and shelter until he could earn some more, but it did not seem an evening for hoarding money.

One and sixpence was not much for an evening out, but it was more than they had been able to put together for some time, so they settled down to make what they could of it. Eight pence went on the cost of admission to the pictures. Moggy was in the mood for entertainment. The atmosphere was warm and smokey and the piano rattled out an endless stream of sound, fast or slow, according to the antics of the jerky little people who cavorted about on the screen. One of Charlie Chaplin's films in particular made him laugh till his side hurt. The other three seemed to get more enjoyment out of watching him doubled up than they did from the comedian.

'Got a fellow feeling with Charlie Chaplin has our Mog,' announced Jan when they left the cinema.

'Both little, ain't they?' said Vicky, nudging Jan in the ribs.

'He ain't so little,' protested Clara.

'Who?' replied Jan. 'Moggy or Charlie Chaplin?'

'He's all right, is Mog. Don't tease him.'

Vicky cocked her head on one side. 'I think he's growing,' she declared. 'Perhaps he'll look down on you before he's finished, Jan.'

For some reason the teasing did not bother Mgogy that evening. Cocking an imaginary hat on his head and swinging an imaginary walking-stick, he waddled off down the street in front of the other three.

'It's quality that counts,' he shouted over his shoulder. 'Back a good little 'un every time.' Once he had won their attention he changed his style and started shadow-boxing at a lamp-post, his head tucked on one side in the manner he had copied from Bob Tranter. He had only managed a couple of passes when his arms became tangled in the sacks which slipped from his shoulder.

'What are you carrying them things for, Mog?' called Vicky.

'I didn't have anywhere to put them,' replied Moggy, his brittle confidence suddenly punctured.

'Might rain,' said Jan, laughing as he looked up at the clear sky, which was not yet quite dark.

'Here, Clara,' shouted Vicky, with a yelp of laughter. 'You'd better watch yourself. Reckon he's brought his bed with him.'

'If he has, he won't get me in it,' replied Clara primly.

'She don't go for sacks, Mog,' teased Jan. 'Nothing but the best sheets.'

Vicky looked at her friend, half seriously. 'Take more than sheets to tempt her.'

'Not like some I know,' said Jan putting out an arm to grasp Vicky.

'You watch it, Jan Jaworski,' she snapped, evading his hand.

The conversation had gone about as far as it would go, and Moggy was thankful at least that the others had not pressed him further on the matter of the sacks.

'We've got tenpence left,' he said hurriedly. 'I'm hungry.'

Fourpence went on four cups of tea; the rest purchased a large bag of chips, into which they dipped in strict rota as they walked slowly along the street.

For Moggy the pleasure had suddenly gone out of the evening. Now they were only putting in time before breaking up for the night. The other three would go off home as usual. A couple of times Moggy almost asked whether there was enough room in any of their houses for him to roll up on the floor, but he had an idea that Jan's family was no better off for space than his. Clara would be bound to take the suggestion wrongly, and he did not know Vicky well enough to ask. At last the girls announced that it was time that they were off. Neither of them had been home since before school in the morning and it was more than time to put in an appearance. Clasping each other round the waist, they set off in the direction of the Mile End Road. Jan was inclined to hang about for a bit longer and Moggy was glad to keep him company for as long as possible. Together they strolled around the alley-ways, but neither of them could find much to say to the other and, at about ten-thirty, Jan decided that he, too, would turn in. He left Moggy at the end of Watney Street, just a couple of turnings away from his home.

The temptation to go back as normal was very powerful. It was the natural, the obvious thing to do. But Moggy pushed the idea from his mind. He knew that nothing would have got any better in the course of the day.

Knowing that he would not sleep before midnight, he decided to take a walk along the river. First he cut through the little alley-ways between Cable Street and the docks. The tall tenements shut out the light of the moon and the few street lamps only cast tiny pools of light beneath each flickering gas mantle.

Slowly he trudged along under the shadow of the blind warehouses which lined Wapping Wall. Then he turned down the Old Steps and stood on the edge of the Thames mud. A sharp wind had blown a bank of cloud over the moon and he could only just make out the distant surface of the water, roughened by sharp little waves.

The tide was as far out as it would go. Moggy remembered that he had heard how, in the old days, they had tied up captured pirates on the stairs at low water and left them to drown in the rising tide.

The traffic on the river was unnaturally still, even for low tide at that time of night. With the wind blowing from the south, the noises of Limehouse on the south bank seemed louder now than those from Wapping behind him. The wind also blew the smells of the river towards him. Rotting sewage and vegetable matter combined to give off a heavy stench, familiar enough but nonetheless unpleasant.

As Moggy watched, the clouds blew away from the moon and the cranes of the Surrey Docks stood out briefly, angular and motionless. Three barges moored off the shore had swung round at right angles to their moorings as the changing tide had slowly swept them through an angle of ninety degrees.

Away on the Surrey Bank the Limehouse Parish Church clock struck the quarter. It must have been somewhat fast, for a full minute passed before the other clocks on both sides of the river echoed it. Slowly Moggy turned and began to climb the steps where, on dark nights long before, terrified pirates had awaited the rising waters.

Most of the inhabitants of Wapping seemed to have gone to sleep in the half hour since he had walked down to the river. Only a few people were in the streets and the majority of those walked silently. There were others besides Moggy who were settling down for a night in the open air. In one or two doorways, outside the range of the street lights, children huddled with their knees tucked up under their chins. They lay in twos, clutching each other for warmth and comfort. At the corner of an alley a man had collapsed, too drunk to find his own way home.

Moggy planned to find himself a warm corner under an arch of the railway which ran just to the north of Cable Street. He found that each of the arches had two or three occupants. Some made it very plain that they had staked out their own territory and would tolerate no intrusions. After trying a number, however, he found one with only a single inhabitant, who was already asleep.

Slowly he prepared for the night. First he loosened the

strings which served as laces for his boots, but he did not take them off altogether for fear of waking up and finding that someone had gone off with them in the night. He laid one of his sacks on the cold stone floor, loosened the collar of his shirt and lay down, pulling his cap under his head and drawing the second sack over his body.

Since moving into the scullery he had become accustomed to sleeping on a hard surface and here, out of the wind, he felt quite warm. A train rattled overhead, no doubt taking late theatre-goers back to their homes to the east of the city. Then it was silent. The accumulated fatigue of many nights overwhelmed him and he was soon asleep.

He had no idea how long he had been unconscious when he was woken by a boot planted firmly in the middle of his back. The beam of a torch shone down into his eyes.

'Move yourself, lad, you can't sleep there.'

As the torch swung away towards the other huddled figure Moggy could make out the outline of a policeman's uniform.

'Bugger off.' The other vagrant yelled at the intruder in a shrill voice.

'Move your bones there. You ain't allowed to sleep here and you know it.'

'What harm are we doing?' growled Moggy as he gathered up his sacks.

'It's the law, ain't it.'

'Thinks we're going to pinch the bleeding railway.' The other occupant of the arch, a shrivelled old man, drew together a heap of newspapers which had served him for a blanket and shuffled off, grumbling as he went. Moggy hung back, reluctant to shift his ground.

'I told you to move yourself, didn't I, boy?' said the policeman sharply.

'Where can I sleep?' asked Moggy.

'Ain't you got no home?'

'No room.'

'Well, you can't lie around like this. I'd get some

lodgings if I was you?'

'What do I use as money?'

'That's your problem, lad. Out of here. Quick, before I boot you out.'

Moggy pulled his cap over his eyes and followed the old man out into the dark. Behind him he heard the policeman talking to his companion, confirming that they had checked all the arches. The children had also been moved from the doorways, and they walked, bleary-eyed, round the street, waiting for the police to pass on so that they could take up their positions for sleep again.

In all Moggy was moved on three times in the course of the night. He discovered that there was no peace on the London streets.

As the hours went by Moggy became gradually more desperate. After the first short period under the railway he never felt remotely like sleeping. As he trudged the streets or huddled in doorways the night stretched interminably on. By the small hours the benefits of the few chips he had eaten with Jan and the girls had long since passed and his stomach felt empty. Although it was the height of summer, the cold began to eat into him, and he wondered how men, women and children managed to stay alive during the dreadful, long winter nights. He recognized nobody else in the streets, except Lushy Sue who shuffled by him when it was just beginning to grow light. She seemed to have grown even older since he had seen her last in the Garden, and the outline of her skull protruded through the folds of grimy skin.

Moggy spent the first hour of daylight propped up against a wall, next to a middle-aged man who seemed well acclimatized to the life.

'Got a bite?' asked the man at last.

'Not a chance,' replied Moggy. 'Could do with something myself.'

'Any tin?'

'Think I'd sleep out if I did?'

'Better get down to the mission hall,' said the man with

a sigh. 'We don't want to be last in the queue.'

'Where's the mission hall, then?' asked Moggy.

'Don't you know?' said the man, surprised. 'It's the only place with a bite for the likes of us. Give you the arse-ache before they feed you, though.'

Moggy did not feel in a mood to worry about the conditions placed on getting the mission's breakfast, so he followed the man as he led the way along the Commercial Road and together they tacked themselves on to the end of the queue which had already formed outside the hall.

A bonneted Hallelujah Lass walked up and down the length of the queue, looking into the faces of the men and women who waited patiently outside the closed door. One or two stared insolently back at her, but most dropped their eyes to their feet or turned their heads to study the brick wall of the mission. Every now and then she stopped to speak. One man had signed on to a ship the week before and she wanted to know why he was not on his way to China. Another was suspected of being drunk; she thrust her head close to his and sniffed the air before interrogating him on how he came to have enough money to get strong drink, but nothing left to buy breakfast like an honest man. Being unable to provide a satisfactory answer, he was ordered out of the queue and sent on his way.

Moggy felt his stomach tighten as she looked him up and down. Out of the corner of his eye he could see that she had a round face, which could be pretty if it were not framed by the ridiculous bonnet, and if the corners of the mouth were allowed to relax a bit.

'Haven't you got a home to go to, lad?'

Moggy felt faintly annoyed at being called a lad by a girl who could not be more than five years older than he was. He shuffled his feet, but did not reply.

'Where do you live?'

'Wapping.'

'Did you sleep out?'

'Fat lot of sleep they let – '

She interrupted him. 'Why not go back home?'

'Because there ain't no room. And there ain't no breakfast neither.'

Moggy turned round and stared ahead, as if to reinforce the fact that he intended to stay and get his breakfast with the rest. The Hallelujah Lass gave him one last glance before continuing her way up the line.

Moggy had grown accustomed in life to waiting, but that morning his head swam through lack of sleep and his legs felt uncertain beneath him. Overhead he could just see the blue of a clear sky through the smoke haze which lay above the roof tops. In the distance he could hear factory hooters announcing the beginning of the day's work – for those who had work to go to.

At last, just before eight o'clock, he heard the sound of the scraping of bolts inside the mission door. Immediately the people straightened up and began to move forwards.

'There's no need to push. All in God's good time,' yelled out the Salvation Army worker. 'Stop that talking,' she shouted, her voice shrill like that of a schoolmistress. 'I'll send you away without your breakfast if you talk.'

At this threat the line fell silent, and they moved forward slowly into the gaunt mission hall. By the time they were all inside, the hall was packed with some five hundred people. Moggy looked round for the promised breakfast, but the others knew the drill. As quickly as possible they arranged themselves in lines and stood silent, with heads bowed.

Several minutes passed before two male officers emerged from a room at the back. They took their time – just like the supervisors at the dock gate. One drew a Bible out of his pocket, while the other surveyed the crowd in front of him. Finally the Hallelujah Lass settled herself down at the harmonium, and all was ready to start.

Moggy half smiled as he remembered wondering how long he would be able to go without singing another hymn. The time had come a good deal sooner than he had expected. They sang a chorus which Moggy had not heard before, but which was obviously well known to the regulars. The words were belted out in the same loud and expressionless manner that the kids used on the last day of term at North Road School. Moggy moved his lips with the rest, but made no attempt to sing. During the reading and the prayer he switched his brain off, as he had learned to switch off during school assembly. But the officers went on a good deal longer than Mr Pender had ever done, and he had never been quite so hungry or tired at the beginning of a school day. Even when the prayer was over, the proceedings were not done. An officer took the opportunity of giving a few well chosen words to his captive audience. God was angry with their many sins, but Christ offered them all forgiveness through repentance. As they took the earthly food offered to them by the mission, they were bidden to remember the heavenly food constantly offered by a loving Saviour.

At last the preliminaries drew to an end and a number of helpers appeared, carrying the earthly food for which they had waited so long.

Two slices of plain bread, one slice of currant bread, a thin wafer of cheese and a mug of water bewitched to look like tea. Moggy was hungry enough to be glad of anything, but he decided there and then that he would rather starve than spend his life waiting in queues for free food. It was well after half past nine before the feeding of the five hundred was complete. Moggy turned to the man who had brought him. They had hardly exchanged more than a couple of dozen words throughout the hours they had waited together.

'I'm off,' he announced.

'You can't go yet,' the man replied.

'Who's stopping me?'

'You've got to stay for the prayer meeting.'

'Prayer meeting! How long does that take?'

'You won't get away for an hour that's for sure.'

'Stuff that! I'm off, I tell you,' snapped Moggy.

'They won't never let you back.'

'I don't want their lousy food.' Moggy stalked across the hall to the door, which was guarded by the Hallelujah Lass.

'Where are you going, my lad?' she asked.

'I ain't your lad and I'm getting out of here.'

One of the male officers, quick to spot the incident, hurried across to help.

'This young man says he's going,' she announced.

'She's dead right at that,' said Moggy.

The officer began to deliver a lecture about gratitude, but Moggy did not let him get into his stride. 'Look, governor,' he said, 'I came here because they told me I'd get something to eat. I'm grateful for what you've given me. All right?'

'The others are grateful enough to stay for the prayer meeting.'

Moggy looked back into the crowded hall. 'Perhaps they've given up hope of getting work. I ain't, if you want to know.'

'What do you do for a living?' asked the officer.

'I'm a docker. If I can get some work I won't need your charity, will I?'

'But everybody who has breakfast—'

'Look, governor,' interrupted Moggy. 'What good's it going to do me, stopping here? Tell me that.'

The officer looked at Moggy and then glanced round to see whether his colleague was watching. 'Go on off, then,' he whispered. Then he turned away quickly into the hall.

The Hallelujah Lass continued to stand blocking Moggy's path. Her eyes stared squarely into his face, as if she was committing every feature to memory.

'Had your eyeful then?' he asked at last. 'The gentleman said I could go.'

'I'm not stopping you,' she replied quietly, moving across ever so slightly so that it was barely possible for him to pass. After pausing for a moment to see whether she would move further, Moggy squeezed by, making sure that his arm did not brush against the fabric of her uniform.

Moggy had no intention of returning home, but for some reason he chose a route which led him by the end of the street. Bet's gang were standing in a circle round two little girls who were performing a complicated dance around some chalk lines. Bet's voice sounded out stridently above the others' as they chanted one of the old East End rhymes:

'As I was going to the fair,
Who should I meet but an old banker there.
The banker's name was Brass,
His old woman's name was old Mother Bottle-Arse,
There was Brass, old mother Bottle-Arse,
There was Whack, old mother Paddy-Whack,
And Johnny and Billy and Teddy,
Oh Liza, lay close to me now.'

Moggy paused in a doorway and then chose a moment when they were clapping their hands at the end of the rhyme to slip across the end of the street. He thought that he had made it without being seen, but he had only walked a few paces when he heard footsteps behind him and Bet slipped her hand into his.

'Where you been, Mog?' she asked.

'Around,' he replied gruffly.

'You all right?'

'As all right as I'm likely to be without no sleep.'

'Come home tonight, Mog. It's better.'

'Did anyone notice I weren't there?' asked Moggy.

'I did.'

'The others?'

'Course they did,' replied Bet without conviction. 'It was all upset this morning,' she added. 'Mum thought her pains was coming.'

'Is the midwife in?'

'It were a false alarm. Can't be long though.'

'It's all we need, ain't it? One more bleeding Harris in the house.'

'You should come home, though, Mog. It's better than being outside. Will you?'

'Not if I can earn enough for a doss I won't.' He pulled his hand free from her grip and walked on down the street, but Bet padded along beside him.

'You won't earn nothing,' she announced. 'Not today.'

'How do you know?'

'Where've you been?' she asked. 'Ain't you heard?'

'Heard what?' he said impatiently.

'They're all on strike.'

'The tally clerks have been out for a week. That's old news.'

'The dockies too,' insisted Bet.

Moggy stopped and looked at his sister. 'How do you know?'

'Everybody knows,' she insisted.

'Where's Dad?' he asked.

'He went out early,' replied Bet. 'Ain't come back yet.'

'Where did he go?'

'St Katherine's, I think. You going to find him?'

'I might try,' he replied. 'See you, kid.'

He ran off down the road which led to the St Katherine's Dock gate. He now noticed that the women were standing in little knots at the doors of their houses, either talking or just looking towards the docks. The streets were as empty of men as they were on the days of the wool-sales when there was work for everybody.

The courtyard in front of the dock gate was more crowded even than it was in the crush before first call, but instead of shouting, swearing and shoving, the men stood absolutely still and silent. The air was electric. The tension was reflected in the grim faces of the pickets standing shoulder to shoulder across the dock gates; it was reflected in the anxious faces of the dock employees, watching proceedings from the safety of the warehouse windows. All attention was riveted on the speaker who was addressing the strikers from a box, immediately in front of the picket line. He was small; almost small enough to be a Harris. But he made up in style for what he lacked in inches. He alone in the sweltering courtyard was in his shirt sleeves, but the sweat was pouring down his face and dark patches of damp stood out on the white cotton of his shirt. A red face was framed by a broad-brimmed hat, perched on the back of his head.

His words gushed out on a tide of emotion. The dockers had been oppressed for too long, he declared. The time had at last come for them to prove to the world that they had the guts to fight for themselves. The docker's leader was angry. He spoke bitterly about the rich who lived idle lives, battening on the labour of others. He spoke bitterly about the respectable members of society who went to church on Sunday in their best clothes, but who, like the Scribe and Pharisee of the parable, crossed over to the other side when they came up against real need. He was even bitter about missionaries, like the Hallelujah Lass who did everything for the poor, except get off their backs. He ranted on against the employers who treated men like inanimate objects – using them when it suited them, and discarding them when it did not. But the most scathing words of all were kept for the class traitors: the black-legs who let down their mates by working when others were on strike.

As if to prove his point he turned and pointed behind his head. The long arm of a crane slowly swung across the grey-blue sky. The men were on strike, but the docks were not idle. Behind the gates men who had broken through the picket line were unloading perishable cargoes.

Moggy climbed on to a ledge on the warehouse wall and looked across the heads of the crowd. He could not pick out his father. The only familiar figure was Fred Keegan, standing at the end of the picket line. As soon as the speaker had finished haranguing the crowd he jumped down from his perch and pushed his way through the crowd.

'Have you seen my dad?' Moggy shouted, tugging at the union man's sleeve.

Keegan looked at him for a moment as if he was a stranger. Then his words came out with an anger that echoed the speaker's. 'Yes I have. The bastard's inside.'

'What do you mean?' gasped Moggy.

'You know bloody well what I mean, kid,' replied Keegan. 'I suppose that mother of yours told him to go to work like a good boy.'

At first Moggy could only hear the hurtful sneer in Keegan's voice. Slowly the meaning of what he was saying dawned on him. His father was a strike breaker, working while his mates were out. By some instinct Moggy sprang to his defence.

'My mum had her pains in the night. He's got to pay the midwife, ain't he?'

'Look, kid,' snapped Keegan. 'I don't give a damn about that. What I say is, bugger a bloke who'll black-leg on his mates.'

Several of the men from the picket line began to crowd around. A lad of about eighteen grabbed Moggy by the jacket and drew him close.

'Scab,' he hissed.

'Take your bleeding mitts off me,' yelled Moggy, pushing the other's hands away. 'I ain't no scab.'

The lad stepped forward, as if to drive Moggy away from the picket line. 'Push off,' he ordered.

Instead of retreating Moggy landed a punch under the lad's heart which stopped him dead in his tracks. It seemed to take him a second or two to realize that the small creature in front of him had no intention of being pushed around.

'I ain't no scab,' repeated Moggy. Then he appealed to Keegan. 'Tell him I ain't done nothing.'

Fred Keegan chose not to intervene. After drawing breath the lad from the picket line launched himself forward. Moggy did not try to box, but fought with everything he had, as he had fought Jan Jaworski in the playground at North Road School. His opponent soon realized that he had taken on more than he bargained for.

Muttering 'bloody scab' under his breath, he tightened up his defences and fought back fiercely.

It was hard to say which of them was getting the better of the scrap when Fred Keegan decided to pull them apart. He looked Moggy coldly in the eye as he held him by the collar of his coat. 'Beat it, kid,' he snapped.

Moggy felt the tears rise in his eyes. He took a swing at Keegan's head, but the union man held him at the end of his long arm, so that the blow passed harmlessly in front of his face.

'I've got a right to be here. I'm a dockie, ain't I?' shouted Moggy. He pointed at the lad from the picket line. 'I told him. I ain't no black-leg.'

'Push off, anyway,' snapped Keegan. 'When you see Curly, you can tell him to keep out of my sight and all.'

'You'll have to close your eyes when you walk through our front door, then, won't you?' jeered Moggy.

'You can move back upstairs any time you like,' retorted Fred Keegan. 'You don't think we'd spend another night in your bloody house, do you?'

'Suit yourselves, I'm sure. Hope those girls of yours enjoy sleeping on the streets. Tell them to give my love to the micks.'

Another speaker had climbed on to the rostrum and the men around were beginning to call for quiet. Moggy wrenched himself free from Keegan's grasp and hurried away round the back of the crowd. He kept his face turned to the wall to hide the tears of anger which now streamed down his face. He was angry at Keegan and at the lad who had picked on him for no reason; but most of all he was angry at his father for being on the other side of the picket line. Soon his lip began to swell and he had a painful bruise on his left shin. He consoled himself with the thought that, if he knew anything about it, the other lad would have a few aches and pains as well.

The new speaker made no attempt to whip up the enthusiasm of the crowd. Talking in a flat tone of voice from prepared notes, he restricted himself to giving information about the stoppage. He explained that the men were in dispute with the management over pay and conditions of work. To prove this he spouted a whole lot of figures, most of which, as far as Moggy was concerned, went straight in one ear and out the other. He was sure that his own hourly rate was buried among all the statistics, but somehow he managed to miss it.

The speaker succeeded in making the whole strike sound deadly dull. He explained that at the moment the dispute lay only with the Port of London Authority, but union officials had gone to the other major ports to try to organize the men there.

Moggy perked up his ears when the man started to talk about strike pay. He admitted that this was a difficult subject as the union funds were very low. Appeals were being sent out to other unions for support. Moggy found it hard to disentangle the hard message from all the union jargon, but, as far as he could understand it, all strikers had to register at union headquarters in the hope that there might be some strike pay around for them to pick up.

If anything, the speech only made Moggy feel even more miserable.

The union men were all standing round the rostrum, trying to look important. It was their day. Come to think of it, mused Moggy, they were rather like army officers; a general had to get involved in a war every now and again to justify his existence. Names like Kitchener and Haig were household words, but nobody would ever have heard of them if they had never had a war to fight. In the same way blokes like Fred Keegan worked for the union, day in, day out and nobody took a blind bit of notice of them. It was only during a strike that they could stand in front of thousands of dockers and look important.

For one wild moment Moggy imagined himself up on the rostrum. He felt sure that, at the very least, he could make a better job of it than the man who was giving out the old rigmarole about pay and conditions of service. Not that Moggy had any rooted objection to speeches about pay!

It was just that it all needed a different slant. Fred Keegan's idea about worker control was a new slant all right, but Moggy doubted whether any of the union men would bring it up in their speeches. The trouble was that none of the dockies would take it seriously.

The men in the courtyard looked as if they would stand, listening to speeches, until the crack of doom. But Moggy felt that he had had enough. He had nowhere special to go and nothing to do, but he could kill time on the streets as well as he could by listening to speeches. He took one last look round the crowded arena and then trudged off on his own.

On normal days Moggy took care not to arrive at the Tranters' house until Bob had had time to wash, change and eat his evening meal. This evening, however, he showed up on the doorstep a full half hour earlier than normal. The ex-boxer looked up at him in surprise.

'Had anything to eat, Mog?'

'Yes. That's all right.'

The fact that he was half starved must have stood out a mile for, without saying anything, Mrs Tranter ladled out a helping of stew and beckoned him into the empty place between them.

'It's all right. Really it is.'

'Take it if she gives it you,' said Bob.

Moggy looked nervously towards Mrs Tranter and smiled his thanks. She was a quiet, composed woman and in the months of calling at the house Moggy did not feel that he had got to know her very well. She seemed happy enough that her husband had revived his interest in boxing, but she never came out to watch the training sessions herself.

'Crikey, you didn't half get through that,' said Bob, when Moggy had cleared his plate. 'You'd better give him some more, Ada.'

This time Moggy did not protest as Mrs Tranter filled his plate. Apart from the mission breakfast he had not had a bite to eat all day and the food was warm and satisfying.

'Got to keep your strength up,' announced Bob. 'I've fixed you another fight Sunday week.'

'Good,' grunted Moggy between mouthfuls.

'Good! I should think it bleeding well is good. You're way up the bill this time.'

Moggy put down his fork and looked across the table at his trainer. 'What do you mean?'

'What I say. I went to the management and said that you was a really promising fighter and it was about time they gave the fans a chance to see you in a proper spot.'

'How much is it worth?' asked Moggy.

'Never stops thinking about money, that one,' declared Ada Tranter.

'Why not?' said Bob. 'Money's what makes the world go round, ain't it?'

'I thought that were love,' replied his wife.

'That's only in the pictures. It's money, ain't it, Mog?' Bob paused as if he was doing a sum in his head, while his eyes teased Moggy. 'Two quid I'd say.'

'Two quid! That must be half way up the bill. The hall'll be bloody packed.'

'Pretty full I should think.'

Mrs Tranter looked across the table at Moggy anxiously. 'Is that wise?' she asked.

'What if I get murdered?' said Moggy. 'I ain't been boxing more than a few months.'

Bob Tranter got up from the table and walked over to the fireplace. 'You could say it's my first big decision as a manager. It's the hardest thing, to know when to hold a man back and when to push him forward. I'll be honest with you. If I had a proper gym and you had the opportunity of fighting against the right sort of opposition, I wouldn't push you so fast. But I reckon you're good, Moggy, and you won't never prove it as long as you go on fighting a few pansy kids down the bottom of the bill.'

Ada Tranter looked non-committally from Moggy to her husband and then rose to pour out the tea. Moggy sat silent, his stomach turning over with the familiar mixture of fear and excitement which always came to him before a fight. He sincerely hoped that it was not going to stay with him for the whole of the next fortnight.

'Hadn't we better get some training in?' Moggy asked restlessly.

'Half a chance, kid. I ain't had my tea yet. We've got all evening.'

Moggy sat impatiently while Bob Tranter lit up a cigarette and sipped at the hot tea. At long last he lifted himself reluctantly to his feet, picked the gloves out of the corner of the room and nodded to Moggy to follow him into the back yard.

It took a full half hour for Moggy to shed his nerves. His body was tense and unrelaxed as he tried too hard to be the kind of fighter with a right to a spot half way up the bill. He was just beginning to get into his stride when Mrs Tranter called out of the back door.

'Someone to see you, Moggy.' She beckoned to a figure skulking in the room behind her. 'You might as well come and see him now you've got this far.'

Charlie Harris appeared hesitantly beside her. He immediately turned his head, as if he did not want to look anyone in the eye. Moggy ran over and put his arm round his brother's shoulder.

'What's the matter, kid?'

As soon as Charlie turned towards him, Moggy could see that his face was puffy and lop-sided with bruises, and his upper lip was cut.

'Who done you over, Charlie?' asked Moggy grimly.

'It don't matter. Loads of them.'

'Have you been home?'

'No. I wanted to see you.'

Mrs Tranter began to wipe the dirt and blood off the boy's face with a damp cloth.

'Has it got around school?' asked Moggy. Charlie nodded.

'What's got around?' asked Tranter.

'Our dad's been working today,' explained Moggy.

'Black-legged, has he?'

'I think it's wicked to pick on a child,' announced Mrs Tranter, as she patted Charlie's injured mouth. 'It ain't his fault what his dad does.'

'That's the way it is,' said her husband. 'You've got to look after yourself in this life.'

Ada Tranter snorted, but she did not try to argue with her husband. She dried Charlie's face carefully and then surveyed her handiwork. 'There you are. You looks like a human being now.'

Bob Tranter slipped the gloves off his own hands and held them out towards Charlie. 'Want a go?'

'Lay off him,' snapped his wife. 'Ain't he had enough for one day?'

'He's got to go back to school tomorrow, ain't he?' replied Bob. 'It's like they say when you've fallen off a horse. You've got to get back on without thinking about it.'

Charlie did not move, so Bob threw the gloves, one after the other, at his midriff. 'Put them on. Moggy won't hurt you. Not much, anyway.'

Charlie looked down at the gloves and then managed a smile. He slipped them on and let Bob tie up the laces.

'They ain't much too big,' he said, surprised.

'I've got small hands,' commented Bob, holding them out in front of him. 'It ain't their size, it's the weight you puts behind them that counts.'

'Come on, then.' With a gloved hand Moggy beckoned Charlie into the middle of the courtyard.

From the moment that Charlie took guard it stood out a mile that he was a natural stylist. While Moggy boxed like an honest worker, Charlie possessed the instincts and reflexes of a true athlete. Bob showed him the proper footwork and within minutes he was moving round the yard on the balls of his feet in a way that Moggy had never been able to master. He also naturally used the classic straight punches, rather than the hooks and uppercuts favoured by his brother.

When they paused for a breather Bob Tranter surveyed his newest pupil with pride. 'He's all right, ain't he, Mog? Give him a couple of years to fill out a bit and I reckon we'll have a champion.'

'He ain't got nothing to worry about tomorrow, that's for sure.'

'That's right,' agreed Bob. 'When they sees he ain't afraid they'll soon give up. You'd better watch his footwork, Moggy. I reckon you could learn a thing or two off your kid brother, you flat-footed old –'

'I can't do it,' protested Moggy. 'The audience would piss themselves if I started doing the fancy stuff.' He tried out a few clumsy dancing steps and then shook his head.

'It don't suit you,' said Charlie. He looked inquiringly at Tranter. 'Shall we go on?'

'There's no stopping him. Go on, then.'

Bob Tranter shot Moggy a meaningful look and nodded. Moggy winked and nodded back. The kid had got the style; there was no doubt about that. Now he only had to try out his nerve. For a time the two brothers circled each other, sparring in a half-hearted manner. Then, without warning, Moggy gave a grunt and waded forwards. Having the advantage over his brother both in strength and experience, he was careful to pull his punches. Charlie tried desperately to hold his style together, but Moggy did not like the way that he closed his eyes and turned his head away when he was afraid of getting hurt.

'That's enough.' Bob Tranter called them apart and put his arm round Charlie's shoulder. 'You've done well, kid. Very well.'

Charlie smiled as he drew off his gloves. 'I was all right, was I?'

'I'm going to make a puggy of you, son.'

'I ain't got nothing to give you,' said Charlie hurriedly.

'Don't worry about that,' Bob assured him. 'You're my long-term investment. You can pay me when you're a champion.'

'Are you going to take it up properly, then?' asked Moggy.

'Yes.' Charlie did not seem quite convinced. 'I expect so.'

Bob Tranter looked from one to the other. 'You both look tired.'

'I didn't get much sleep last night,' confessed Moggy.

'Are you coming home?' asked Charlie.

'Not unless the Keegans have gone.'

'I saw Bet,' said Charlie. 'She told me. They moved out at tea-time. Mum paid two men to move the big bed upstairs again. Swearing blue murder you weren't there to help, she was.'

'Anything happening?'

'What about?' asked Charlie, puzzled.

'The baby, of course.'

'Bet said it was born at four o'clock this afternoon. It's a girl. Only took half an hour. They just got the bed upstairs in time.'

'She's had some practice, your mum,' put in Bob.

'Don't know why she goes on,' Moggy thought it over. 'Can we sleep in the front room again?'

'I don't see why not,' replied Charlie.

'I suppose I might as well come back, then. For tonight, anyway.'

Charlie's face broke into a smile. 'I hoped you'd come back, Mog,' he said. 'That's why I came to find you.'

Charlie's spirits had completely revived by the time that the two of them set off for home. Moggy had to admit to himself that, had he been in his brother's shoes, he would have felt scared at the thought of returning to school next day. But the boxing and Bob Tranter's praise for his classic style seemed to have given him a full measure of confidence. Moggy was not sure that the skills which he had been practising would be much use if the other boys chose to set on him again. But the important thing was that he now felt as though he could look after himself. Moggy knew from long experience that what Bob had said was true. The bullies in North Road School only picked on the kids who showed that they were afraid. Confidence was everything, and it was good to see his young brother's confidence so well and truly repaired.

They talked nothing but boxing as they walked through the darkening streets. Moggy tried to measure from his brother's conversation whether he had responded to Bob Tranter's talk about a professional career seriously. Moggy was pretty sure that Bob had meant it seriously enough. But Charlie did not talk about boxing as if it were his life's ambition. He seemed much more concerned with weighing up which of the larger boys in his year at school he would now be able to take on.

When they were within sight of their home Moggy's brain was far removed from the subject of the strike and his father's black-legging. It therefore took some time before the four letters painted on the front wall of the house formed themselves into a word.

'What's that?' asked Charlie, stopping still in the middle of the road.

For a time Moggy did not reply. He bit on the laces of his gloves as the anger rose inside. 'You can read. You can read what it bloody well says as well as I can.'

'S-C-A-B.' Charlie spelt out the letters one by one.

'Brilliant!' Moggy's voice was bitter with sarcasm. 'S-C-A-B spells scab. That's what our dad is, remember.'

Charlie walked forward and tried the paint with his finger. 'It's still wet.'

'Get me something to rub it off with.'

'You'll make one hell of a mess.'

'Look,' shouted Moggy, 'I don't give a bugger. It'll be dry in a minute. I ain't living in a house with "scab" written all over it.'

Charlie looked vaguely in the gutters to see whether there was a rag lying about.

'Get something from inside,' ordered Moggy. 'There's a bloody great pile of sacks inside the door.'

Moggy fretted while Charlie pushed open the door of the house and disappeared indoors. When he reappeared he was playing tug-of-war with his father over the possession of a sack.

'I asked what you wanted it for, didn't I?' bellowed Mr Harris.

With a sudden jerk, Charlie tore the other end out of his father's hand. 'Here you are, Mog,' he called as he hurled it towards his brother.

Moggy caught the sack and immediately started rubbing at the letter S.

'What in Christ's name are you doing?' demanded his father.

'I'm painting the house, can't you see.'

'No you're not.'

'Ask a silly question, get a silly answer.'

Mr Harris was about to lunge forward for the sack, but he froze in his tracks as he read the four letters on the wall.

'I hadn't seen,' he said quietly.

The sarcasm returned to Moggy's voice. 'Didn't they knock on the door and ask your permission before they painted it? Got no manners, some people.'

'Hey,' said Mr Harris. 'Ain't you rubbing the paint into the brick?'

'It won't never come off now, Mog,' put in Charlie.

Moggy spun round and thrust the sack towards his father. 'You want to leave it there? Tell all the neighbours. Remind them in bloody years to come.' When his father did not answer he turned back to his task and went on rubbing until the letters had been reduced to a huge, indecipherable smudge across the front of the house. He then threw the sack down on to the pavement and walked in through the open door, with Charlie and his father behind him.

'I thought you'd left us,' said Mr Harris.

'The Keegans went off, didn't they? I presume I can have my old place back.'

'Suit yourself,' said his father. 'I just thought you might feel the same way as Fred. You are on strike, aren't you?'

'Look,' declared Moggy. 'Everyone's on strike. Everyone except you, that is.'

'All right Mister High and Mighty. Someone had to pay the midwife. I didn't notice that you contributed anything.'

'I'll bet you that Fred Keegan wouldn't have gone to work, even if his missus was having triplets.'

'Well, I ain't Fred Keegan, and that's all there is to it,' snapped Mr Harris.

'What did they pay you: double time?'

Mr Harris did not answer, but a smirk formed round his mouth. Moggy looked at him, amazed.

'More than double time? You cunning sod. How much did you do?'

'Thirteen hours.'

'Thirteen hours at more than –' Moggy did a mental sum. ' – You didn't have to hand over all that to the midwife. Jesus, you'll be a millionaire by the end of the week – if you live that long. Still, you'll probably be all right.'

'What do you mean, I'll be all right?'

'I shouldn't think they'll bother with you. It's Charlie'll catch it.'

'Charlie?'

'Yes, Charlie. Didn't you notice? Take a gander at his phiz.'

The boy had already unrolled his mattress and was settling down to sleep. The swelling had subsided considerably, but, with his face in repose, the bruises stood out livid.

'What happened?' asked Mr Harris.

'What the bleeding hell do you think happened? They duffed him up, that's what. Because he was your kid.'

Curly Harris knelt beside the mattress and ran his hand through Charlie's hair. 'Are you all right, lad?'

The boy's eyes had closed and he did not show any sign of having heard.

'He's done in,' said Moggy. 'Bob Tranter and I thought

we'd better teach him how to look after himself. He'll need to if you keep going to work.'

Mr Harris looked down at his sleeping son. 'I won't make it worse for him.'

'What're you going to do tomorrow, then?' asked Moggy pointedly.

'If you want to know, I'm going to go out and get stoned out of my mind. It's as good a thing to do as anything, ain't it?'

'You earned the money.'

'Don't worry,' said Curly Harris. 'I won't offer you any. It'd be against your principles to take bosses' money, I'm sure.'

'Try me and see.'

'What're you going to do?'

'Me?' asked Moggy. 'I hadn't thought. I might join the pickets.'

'Remember, you won't bring in the revolution that way,' teased his father.

'It's something to do,' replied Moggy.

Mr Harris made to go upstairs and then checked himself. 'Do you want to see the baby?' he asked.

Moggy pulled out his mattress and unrolled it on the floor. 'She'll be there in the morning, won't she? Another ruddy woman! One thing; she won't never be a dockie. What a bleeding life.'

'There's worse,' said his father.

'Always look on the flaming bright side. That's what I like about you.'

Mr Harris half smiled at Moggy. 'Just because you're a miserable sod! I'm going to get my head down.'

From upstairs came the thin sound of a new baby crying. Curly Harris looked up towards it and winced.

'Better keep off it for a year or two,' suggested Moggy. 'Give us all a chance of a bit of shut-eye at night.'

'That mother of yours'd get a bun in the oven even if I sat opposite her at the dinner table. One thing – I don't have to get up in the morning.'

'You really ain't going to work?' pressed Moggy suspiciously.

'Don't you believe nothing I say? I tell you, I ain't going to move a muscle till the pubs open. Anyway – ' he looked down at Moggy – 'you'd make sure I didn't get through the dock gates even if I did change my mind, wouldn't you?'

Moggy sized his father up. 'Reckon I could sort you out.'

'Oh, yes,' said Curly Harris. 'I forgot you was a fighter. Still, I wouldn't bank on it, sonny; not if I was you.'

7

It was soon very clear to Moggy that the strike had little chance of succeeding. In the first place the other ports did not come out in sympathy, as had been hoped. London was certainly the hub of the nation's trade and people got hot under the collar about perishable cargoes rotting on the wharfs of Wapping and Limehouse. After the first week shoppers in the London area began to find that some goods were unobtainable but, with goods being landed every day at a dozen other ports around the country, nobody was exactly in danger of starving. Nobody, that was, except the dockers themselves! The union leaders grumbled that, if all the men had paid their subscriptions regularly there would have been enough money in the kitty to keep up a proper level of strike pay.

The thirteen hours' extra pay which Curly Harris had earned through black-legging had gone within two days. Being laid up in bed with the new baby, Mrs Harris did not succeed in laying her hands on any of it. Mr Harris managed to produce a shilling every now and then with which Bet bought bread, tea and a few vegetables for the family, but that was all. For the first week Moggy and his father both got a shilling a day strike pay, which helped, and Mr Pender's bread and treacle saw Charlie and Bet through the morning at school.

Within a few days public opinion had moved firmly against the strike. In normal times the national newspapers never bothered to cover events at the docks. None of them, for instance, had kept their readers informed about the unemployment and hardship of the summer months. But as soon as a few items were in short supply in the West End shops, reporters trooped out of Fleet Street to check up on what was happening. They buzzed like flies around

Moggy's picket by the gate of the London Dock, which was nearest to the city. They were always asking questions about the strike. In particular they were concerned to find out whether the men knew just what they were striking about. Moggy could have filled them in on quite a few things which he had discovered about the life in his first four months as a dockie, but he knew that none of them would take a blind bit of notice. They seemed only interested in facts and figures about conditions of service and bonus payments for different categories of dirty cargoes. In the end Moggy always ended up by telling them to get lost.

The union man who organized Moggy's section of the picket had all the answers. Since he could spout facts and figures like a gramophone record, the men left him to do the talking for them. The reporters seemed to find this suspicious and they printed articles in which they said that ignorant and innocent workers were being led astray by irresponsible union leaders.

To Moggy, the union man seemed responsible to the point of absurdity. He was always going on about the fact that they could not afford to lose public sympathy and he took pride in the fact that his sector of the line was disciplined and orderly. Every now and then they heard of fights and scuffles in other parts of dockland, but for the first week the picket on the London Docks was a model of good order and discipline.

Later on Moggy always insisted that it was the bosses who were really responsible for the change in temper in the second week. It was easy enough for the official to keep his men in order as long as nobody tried to cross their line. It was only natural, however, that when the bosses decided to get tough, the men were prepared to play the same game. The newspapers in particular seemed determined to stir up trouble. After the strike had been going on for a week editors began to vie with each other to see which could write the strongest leading articles. Some even urged the government to put in troops and move the goods which had been lying on the wharf side since the beginning of the strike. Rumours passed around dockland that the army could be expected to appear on the scene at any moment.

Moggy did not set eyes on Fred Keegan after the first day of the strike, but he could not help wondering how the union man felt that things were going. He wondered in particular whether he retained his touching faith in the fact that soldiers were working men who, when it came to the point, would not fight against their own kind. Whichever way one looked at it, thought Moggy, he and his mates were in a spot. They were not big enough fools to think that the dockies were going to come out of the strike with control over the Port of London. Whether they liked it or not the stoppage was about a copper or two on the hourly rate and the odd improvement in working conditions. The bosses on their side had spotted that the strike was shaky. The union could not go on dishing out strike pay and the dockers themselves had run through any reserves they might have had and pawned anything worth pawning during the bad weeks in June and July. The bosses therefore decided to pile on the heat. They were determined to move goods through the picket lines, whether the men liked it or not. They had already lined up police escorts and, if the papers were anything to go by, they would soon have the army out as well.

The Fred Keegans in the union had got to make up their minds; either they must let the men tangle with the law – even if it meant that a few people would get hurt – or they had to accept the fact that they were on a beating and get out of the strike, saving as much face as they could manage.

Moggy tried to argue it out with the union official who was responsible for the picket on the London Dock, but the man either did not understand what Moggy was talking about – or pretended that he did not understand. He explained that the union had laid down a procedure to be followed when anyone tried to move goods through the dock gate. The pickets were to sit down on the ground and refuse to move until they were forcibly dragged away. They were to use every possible means of preventing anything from coming through – short of actual physical violence.

All the other men accepted the instructions without protest, and Moggy did not feel that it was his place, as the youngest there, to argue the toss. They would in all probability have followed instructions to the letter if the outsiders had not chosen to join the picket line on the very day that the bosses decided to shift goods through the main gate of the London Dock.

Moggy did not realize that the newcomers were in fact intruders until he recognized Jan Jaworski among them.

'Here, Jan,' called Moggy.

He had to call three times before Jan spotted him and came over to talk.

'What're you doing here?' asked Moggy.

'I heard you needed some help,' replied the Pole.

'Who's this?' The union official had bustled over and pointed an accusing finger at Jan.

'Friend of mine,' replied Moggy.

'Is he a union member?'

'Course I am,' replied Jan insolently. 'Ain't I, Mog?'

'That's right,' said Moggy.

Jan looked along the line at his friends. 'We're all members of the union.'

The official looked at him uncertainly and pulled himself up, like a football referee about to send an offending player off the pitch.

Jan's face took on a look of hurt innocence. 'Straight up, governor,' he protested. He fumbled in his pocket. 'I've left my card behind.'

Moggy did not think that the official had been taken in, but he was obviously reluctant to get involved in a trial of strength. It was easy enough to tell Jan and his friends that they had to go, but it was a great deal harder to make sure that they actually went. 'If you want to stay, make sure you obey the rules.' He turned to Moggy. 'You're responsible. See that he understands.'

As the official walked down the line Moggy started to explain the agreed procedure to Jan.

'Oh, stuff it, Mog,' said Jan. 'I ain't seen you. Where've you been hiding?'

'I've been around,' replied Moggy briefly.

'Seen Clara?'

'I did Sunday.'

'You won't keep her happy unless you look after her better than that,' teased Jan.

'Look,' snapped Moggy. 'I ain't that bothered, am I?'

'Got another bit of skirt, then?'

'Shut your –'

'Work out all your energies in the ring, do you?' Jan nudged Moggy but he could see clearly enough from his face that he was not in a mood for joking. He quickly changed his tone of voice. 'Still boxing?' he asked.

Moggy nodded. 'On and off.'

'When's the next fight? I must come and see the man in action.'

'Next Sunday.'

'Doing all right, are you?'

'Not bad – for a junior.'

'How long have you been at it?'

'Three months,' replied Moggy. 'I stand to win two quid this time.'

'I'd fight you for two quid.'

Moggy looked Jan up and down. 'I ain't fighting you. Not again.'

'I might take it up,' said Jan. 'When I'm in the army.'

'You're not still after that racket?'

'Why not? I told you, it's all right.' Jan nudged Moggy in the ribs. 'Wait till I'm in a flash uniform, matey.'

'Have to fight the tarts off, will you?'

'O.K., laugh. There's something sexy about them togs. You've got to admit it.'

'I still don't get why you want to be a bloody soldier,' declared Moggy.

'You wouldn't, Mog. It's the life. I couldn't fester away in this dump. Bleeding docks!'

'They're going to be better, ain't they?'

'When?'

'After the strike.'

'That's a laugh!' said Jan harshly. 'You're a poor, bloody sod if you think you're going to get anything out of this lot.'

'What're you here for, then?'

'The action, boy. A soldier's got to be where the action is.'

Moggy looked him up and down. 'Soldier. Christ!'

'What's wrong?' asked Jan.

'The soldiers are on the other bleeding side, remember?'

'O.K., so the next strike maybe I'll be on the other side. I'd soon fix you lot. Look. I could sort out this strike quicker than that. No bloody guts to it.'

'So they'll make you a general to show them how.' Moggy tensed as he heard a noise from inside the dock gates.

'What's that?' asked Jan.

'A cart. They're bringing the stuff through.'

'Going to stop them?'

'They won't get it through that easy,' replied Moggy.

The union official bustled along the picket, checking that the men were in their places. Jan stood beside Moggy, looking straight to the front as the official walked past. Then he turned and signalled to the other newcomers who had also taken their places in the line.

A key sounded in the lock and slowly the dock gate opened. Three carts, laden and covered by tarpaulins stood waiting to come through. They were guarded by some thirty policemen. At a signal from the union official the men on picket duty sat down in a line across the gate. Moggy had to drag Jan down beside him. The sergeant of police stepped forward and delivered the routine instructions to the men to clear the road before they were forcibly removed.

'What do we do?' asked Jan.

'We sit,' explained Moggy.

'Stuff that,' exclaimed Jan.

'Every time they release you, just sit down again,' insisted Moggy.

'What good does that do?' asked Jan.

'Holds them up.'

'What in Christ's name's the use of that?' repeated Jan. 'You're here to stop them, ain't you?'

A burly policeman grabbed both Moggy and Jan by the backs of their collars and dragged them roughly across the cobbles.

'You stay there, lads,' he ordered as he deposited them at the side of the yard.

Jan leapt to his feet and put his face close to the policeman. 'You can't treat –' His protest was cut short by a blow across the side of the face, which sent him spinning back on to the ground.

By the time that Jan had recovered the other outsiders had already moved into action. A group of them had got their shoulders under the side of the leading cart and were rocking it until it began to topple dangerously. The policemen went swiftly into action, pulling first one and then another away from the cart.

For a time the dockers from the picket line watched passively while the outsiders struggled to overturn the cart. Then one by one they leapt from the ground to take the places of those who were pulled away. Despite the frantic efforts of the police, the cart swayed even more dangerously. Moggy caught a glimpse of the driver's face – mouth open and hands in the air – just before he was thrown headlong off his seat. From the other side of the yard he could even hear the crack as the man's arm broke when he hit the cobbles.

Jan shook his head to clear it and then took a curved object out of his pocket. 'Come on, Mog,' he called. 'Let's sort the bastards.'

The union official made a futile attempt to stop Jan and Moggy as they ran towards the second cart. The driver had already deserted his post and was scurrying back towards the wharf. The police were now fully occupied trying to fight back a crowd of women and children which had gathered out of nowhere and was bent on gathering the one pound packets of butter which had fallen off the first cart and lay scattered all over the courtyard.

Jan leapt on to the second cart and threw a rope down to Moggy. 'Untie that,' he yelled. 'We'll ditch this lot too.' With a single stroke from the object which he carried he ripped the tarpaulin wide open. Moggy managed to loosen one corner of the rope, and together they managed to tear open the rear portion of the load.

'This one's butter too,' shouted Moggy. 'What do we do?'

'We see that it ain't fit to eat,' replied Jan. As quickly as he could he started to scoop the packets on to the ground. Once there he systematically dug his heel into each. Soon they were joined by others who helped them with the task.

They had shifted half the load when they heard a whistle blowing in the courtyard behind them. Moggy turned round in time to see the police sergeant calling to his men. They regrouped around him and took the batons out of the slings at their belts. At the sight of the sticks the women and children swiftly retreated to a safe distance. The sergeant shouted instructions to his men; they fanned out across the yard, and then charged forward with their batons held high in the air.

Those with quick enough wits chose that moment to slip away. Jan paused long enough to hurl three pounds of butter at the on-coming policemen. Then he put his arm round Moggy's waist.

'I'm off, kid,' he panted.

It did not even occur to Moggy that he could get away

as well. Out of the corner of his eye he saw Jan dodge out of the way of a policeman's baton and then run towards the watching crowd.

The police swung their batons from side to side, in long, ferocious arcs. Moggy just managed to thrust his forearm in the way of a full blow aimed at his skull before pitching himself into a blue midriff. The policeman went over like a felled tree and his truncheon clattered on to the cobbles. Desperately Moggy dived after it, but he could not move fast enough. Another policeman hit him when he was still several feet from his objective. This time Moggy had not seen the blow coming and he took the whole force on his left shoulder. He pitched forward on to his face and covered his head with his arms as blows continued to fall across his back. Through watering eyes he could just make out the shape of a blue pair of trousers; he lashed out at them with his boots. At the same time he tried to heave himself back on to his feet, but no sooner had he struggled on to his knees than he was knocked back on to the cobbles again. This time he chose to lie still and to his relief the policemen which had been hitting him ran off to assist their colleague. By the time that Moggy dared to open his eyes the sergeant was bringing the situation under control once again. About twenty of the pickets and two or three policemen looked quite badly hurt. Moggy's back and shoulders ached fiercely, but mercifully his head had escaped punishment. One of the policemen hauled him to his feet.

'Right, you little bastard,' he said. 'You come with me.'

With a sharp movement he twisted Moggy's arm behind his back so that he could not struggle while being searched.

'What's this?' asked the policeman, drawing a meat-hook out of his right-hand pocket.

Moggy looked at it in disbelief. 'It ain't mine,' he gasped.

'Not yours?' sneered the policeman. 'How did it get in there then?'

Moggy realized with a surge of anger that Jan must have slipped it into his pocket before he ran off. He started to explain but checked himself in time. 'I don't know,' he muttered.

The policeman examined the hook with his finger. The points were sharp and one of the inner edges had been filed down to form a rough cutting edge, which had sliced through the tarpaulin.

'Nasty,' he said. 'Very nasty.' His voice was quiet but menacing. 'Still say it isn't yours?'

'That's right.'

With a swift movement the policeman swung a blow to the side of Moggy's face, but Moggy reacted fast enough to duck so that it only grazed the top of his head. The policeman shaped up for a second blow, but thought better of it as he caught sight of the sergeant out of the corner of his eye. Without releasing the pressure on Moggy's arm he propelled him across the courtyard.

The sergeant examined the meat-hook and then looked Moggy over from head to foot. 'I ought to do you, kid,' he said. 'Carrying an offensive weapon. Assault. It's good for Borstal.' He studied Moggy with eyes that were half amused, half malicious. 'I can fix you easier than that.' The sergeant called out to a supervisor who had emerged from the dock gate to survey the ruins of the two loads of butter. 'Come over here. I've got something to show you.'

The supervisor took one last rueful look at the mess and walked across. 'What is it?' he asked.

'Ever seen this chap?' asked the sergeant.

Moggy had seen the supervisor once or twice, but he had never worked in one of his gangs so he did not expect to be recognized.

'I don't know,' replied the supervisor. 'Looks a bit familiar.'

'Give him your card, boy,' snapped the sergeant.

Moggy handed his docker's card to the supervisor who studied it with maddening deliberation. 'Morgan Harris.' A ray of light crossed his face. 'You Curly Harris's kid?'

'That's right,' agreed Moggy.

'You look like him. That's why I thought I'd seen you.'

He turned to the sergeant. 'Steady man, Harris.'

'I don't know anything about his father,' said the sergeant, 'but I know a few things about this one.' He shoved the hook into the supervisor's hand. 'Nice looking object, isn't it?'

The supervisor looked at the hook with distaste. 'This yours?'

'No, it ain't,' protested Moggy.

'Where did you find it?' the sergeant asked the policeman who had brought him over.

'In his pocket.' He pointed to the right side of Moggy's jacket. 'That one.'

'Are you accusing the constable of planting it on you?' the sergeant asked sharply.

'No,' admitted Moggy. Then he added again, 'But it ain't mine.'

'Just borrowed it, did you?' asked the supervisor with a sneer.

'Perhaps he found it lying about,' suggested the policeman.

Moggy realized that it was hopeless to protest. They would never believe him unless he was prepared to shop Jan Jaworski, and the unwritten laws of dockland made that impossible.

'Have I got to charge him?' asked the sergeant meaningfully.

'It doesn't seem necessary, does it?' replied the supervisor. 'Your dad'll be ashamed of you when he hears.' He paused for a moment as if expecting Moggy to say something. Then he added, 'Don't come back, sonny.'

'What do you mean?' asked Moggy quickly.

Again, with maddening deliberation, the supervisor began to tear Moggy's card into pieces. First he shredded it longways, then he finished the job by reducing the pieces to the size of confetti. When he had finished he put them on to the palm of his right hand and blew the pieces into the air.

'It's simple,' he said at last. 'Don't come back here, or to any of the docks. If you do you'll be wasting your time. I'll see you don't get any work.'

'You'll black me?' asked Moggy, unbelieving.

'You've got the idea, kid,' replied the supervisor. 'There won't be a supervisor in the Pool who doesn't know the name Morgan Harris.' The supervisor tried the name out a second time. 'Morgan. I'll bet your mates don't use a jaw-breaker like that. What do they call you?'

'My name's Morgan,' growled Moggy. He pointed at the pieces of paper on the cobbles. 'Like it said on that.'

'Well bugger off, then, Morgan.' The sergeant grinned maliciously as he wrung full value out of the name. 'Don't let me clap eyes on you again or I swear I'll have you put inside. And you won't get out in a hurry, either.'

Moggy looked from one to the other as if he wanted to argue the toss, but it was obviously useless. Slowly he turned and walked away in the direction that Jan had disappeared, flattening a couple of pounds of butter with the soles of his boots as he went.

The early contests on the bill at Premierland seemed to go on for ever. Moggy had not known what time he had to present himself at the hall, but he felt he had better be on the safe side and assume that all the bouts would end with a knock out in the first round. In point of fact all but one of them went the full distance. Bet, who sat on one side of him, was restless and bored. On the other side Charlie sat slouched in his seat watching the fighters through narrowed eyes. Moggy could not make out whether he was studying them to pick up useful tips, or whether he was as bored as Bet and just showing it in a different way.

Moggy's own nerves were on edge. Every few moments he looked round to see how the hall was filling up and he began to realize that, as Bob Tranter had forecast, he would be fighting in front of a full house. It suddenly seemed crazy that Bob should have pressed for him to be given such a high spot on the programme.

When Bob had first told him about the fight he had been excited; he had wanted to win. Now he knew that he had to win. The strike had folded at the end of its second week. The management had given way on one or two minor points, but none of the dockers could kid themselves that they had won. The men were due back at work on Monday. Mr Harris was looking forward to things being normal again, and Moggy had not got round to telling him that he was going to be out of a job. It was a funny thing, but he felt quite cut up about it all. He did not enjoy waiting in a heaving mass of humanity at the dock gate, but in an odd way he was going to miss it. In the few months since leaving school Moggy had got used to the idea of being a dockie. It sounded ridiculous, but he had a feeling that, if he had stayed on, he might even have got tied up with the union himself.

Ideas and anxieties went round and round in Moggy's brain as he tried to concentrate on the early bouts. At last he nudged the pair on either side of him.

'Time for off.'

'Is it you now?' asked Bet, perking up.

'Next but one.'

'Good luck, Mog,' said Charlie, coming out of his trance.

'I'll need it, kid.'

Moggy scooped up his kit and picked his way over the spectators' legs towards the competitors' exit. The changing room was half full, and Moggy made no attempt to guess which was to be his opponent. Swiftly he changed into his kit and then sat down to wait. Before long Bob Tranter came in to make sure that all was well. He checked Moggy's gloves and the soles of his shoes, but made no attempt to talk or offer any advice. When at last the bout was called, he just gave Moggy a playful cuff round the ear before following him out into the hall.

It appeared to Moggy that the crowd had grown larger and more noisy even during the short time that he had been in the changing room. He could not distinguish individual voices, only a jarring buzz which increased in volume as he ducked under the ropes and sat down in his corner. As he looked across the ring at his opponent the edginess and nerves fell away from him. He was conscious of Bob Tranter whispering in his ear and then he heard the voice of the master of ceremonies announcing the fight. But the individual words were just a meaningless jumble of syllables. He never heard his opponent's name or weight, or where he came from. He only knew that he was a swarthy-looking lad, perhaps a couple of years older than he was, with tattoo marks up both arms and across his shoulders. His dark hair was slicked down with grease, away from his eyes, and there was the beginnings of a moustache above his lip.

Moggy rose automatically to his feet as the bell went and stepped forward to where the referee waited for them in the centre of the ring. The referee muttered a few words, they touched gloves, and the fight had begun.

Moggy was quite unprepared for the speed with which his swarthy opponent took the fight to him. Most boxers liked to start quietly while they sized up the situation, but this one did not pause for a moment. Punches from both hands rained on Moggy's head and body, until he staggered backwards against the ropes and covered up to save himself from further punishment. When he opened his eyes he caught a glimpse of his opponent's face, impassive and cold, the lip with the moustache curling and uncurling in a regular rhythm. Desperately Moggy plunged forward, until their arms were intertwined and their heads rested on each other's shoulder.

'Break.'

The referee stepped in to prise them apart. The moment they disengaged the other boxer's fists swung into action. Still his face showed no emotion, and the lip kept on working up and down. Moggy was dazed and hurt and he felt the familiar sensation of blood flowing across his lips and on to his chin.

'Wash your nose, Mog, your chin's bleeding.'

Moggy remembered the taunt of the kid in the playground of North Road School. He could not hear the individual voices of the Premierland crowd, but the total sound had a baying quality – like the sound of the music hall audience when the girl was trying to sing her stupid song. They had sensed drama – a quick finish – and they were egging on their man to a speedy kill.

Moggy dodged and wove to keep out of trouble as best he could, and after about a minute and a half his opponent relaxed the onslaught to recover his breath. Moggy's instinct told him that the moment had come for him to launch his counter attack, but his arms and legs refused to do what they were told. The crowd seemed angry at the delay and yelled for the action to begin again. Moggy could feel the blood pumping out of his nose and realized that he must look a beaten man. But slowly, as his breath returned, he began to waddle forward in his flat-footed style, trying to bore past the tattooed arms to his opponent's body. At last, just before the bell rang for the end of the round, he managed to land just one solid punch. It did not go far towards making up for all the punches which had been showered around his own body. He had lost the round by the widest possible margin, but at least he had opened the scoring on his own account. If he had landed one punch he could land more.

It was quickly obvious that Bob Tranter had given up hope. He gave all sorts of good advice as he mopped the blood from Moggy's face and body, but his voice carried no conviction. Deep down he was swearing at himself for putting Moggy into the senior bouts before he was ready. Perhaps, thought Moggy, he was wondering whether he would have better luck with Charlie than he had had with his older brother.

Moggy swilled out his mouth and spat pink water into the sand tray. As he did so he shut his ears to Bob's voice and fixed his eyes across the ring at his opponent. Somehow he just had to find some way to beat the dark-haired boxer. He had nothing against him as a man. When it came down to it, thought Moggy, he was just another geezer trying to earn a living. But he had to win, even if there was not a soul in the hall who thought that he could do it.

Moggy was braced and ready for the flurry of punches which greeted him as soon as they were in the centre of the ring for the second round. Within a few moments his nose was bleeding again, and to the audience it must have appeared as though the pattern of the first round was being repeated.

'Finish him off. Finish him off.'

Moggy could not hear the words but the whole crowd seemed to be shouting in unison for his downfall. The fists were fast and Moggy had no hope of parrying all the combination punches which rained on to him, but he rode as many as he could as he shuffled forward into the scrap.

Whatever the crowd might have thought, Moggy himself knew that there was the world of difference between the first round and the second. In the first his opponent had had all the initiative. In the second round Moggy's brain was as cold as ice. As he watched the little moustache curl and uncurl, Moggy tried to assess how the round would go. If the first was anything to go by, his man would take a breather about half way through.

Licking the blood off his lips Moggy watched for the first sign of relaxation. At last he spotted it – little more than a slight sagging, a slowing down of the rate at which the upper lip pumped upwards and downwards. With a spasm of energy Moggy hurled himself on to his opponent. His fists flailed frantically as he did everything in his power to regain the initiative and turn the tide of the fight.

Both the crowd and the other boxer seemed to be taken by surprise. To them Moggy was just so much dead meat and everyone was waiting for the carve-up. At first they appeared to resent his presumption, but then Moggy heard a few cheers which he knew by instinct were meant for him.

Moggy's assault was hardly elegant, but at least it was effective. His opponent ducked to cover up his face and the two boxers' heads met with a crack which could be heard at the back of the hall. Moggy's brain swam and for a moment he thought that he would go down on to the canvas, but he leant on his opponent to give support to his sagging knees and for a moment he could taste the grease off the other man's hair.

'Break.'

As they staggered apart Moggy could see that his opponent's face and shoulders were covered with blood. Most of it had originated from Moggy's own nose, but a thin trickle was coming from a narrow cut above the man's bushy left eyebrow.

Moggy had heard Bob Tranter's talk about the cuts above the eye which were the bane of every boxer's life, but he had never had first-hand experience of them before. Instinctively he felt sorry for his dark, tattooed opponent. For the first round and a half he must have thought that he had the fight sewn up, but now the odds were more even and the outcome less sure.

Without pausing to clear his own head Moggy threw himself forward. He landed a short left to his opponent's stomach, which brought his head down with a jerk, and then carried his right round in a hook, straight on to the damaged eye. When they separated Moggy could see that he had opened the cut considerably wider and the blood was beginning to flow. Without waiting Moggy went in yet again, driving all his punches towards the ever-widening cut.

The moustache had now stopped moving and the man's lips were drawn back tight across his teeth. Several times he tried to defend himself by taking the fight back to Moggy, but he seemed to sense that the fates had decided against him. As Moggy attacked again and again in the closing minute of the round he could hear the noise of the crowd rising in his ears. They were baying him on, calling for blood.

With the sound of the bell Moggy walked back to his corner to the sound of applause. Bob Tranter was waiting for him, his face almost sad.

'The referee ought to have stopped it. His eye's wide open.'

Moggy could see that Bob Tranter disliked the way that he had worked on the injured eye. There were some who thought that it was better form to leave the damaged bits of an opponent alone, but Moggy did not go along with that. His job as a fighter was to win; the referee was there to see that he did it fairly. He was sorry for the other man, but that was how it was, and that was how he expected it to be if at any time he was on the receiving end.

The interval was a formality. Nobody expected the other boxer to come out of his corner for a third round and, sure enough, Moggy was declared the winner on a technical knock-out. When he went over to his opponent's corner, for the first time the tattooed man smiled at him.

'I thought I'd got you,' he said wryly.

'I hope it mends,' said Moggy.

'Yes; yes,' said the other man abstractedly. 'I hope so.'

After being cleaned up, the cut looked wide and livid and Moggy wondered whether the scar would ever heal properly. Perhaps, he thought, his own career would one day end on just such an anti-climax. In the meantime, however, he had two pounds to collect. Perhaps, with a bit of luck, he would be able to put together a good bit more before anything drastic happened to him.

By the time that Moggy rejoined Bet and Charlie in the body of the hall he had two pound notes safely stowed away in his trouser pocket.

'Don't do that to me,' said Bet. 'Give me heart failure, you did.'

'Think he had me, did you?'

'Everyone did. We thought we was going to have to carry you home, didn't we, Charlie?'

Charlie nodded but did not speak so Bet prattled on, 'You really looked done for till he got that cut on his eye. I don't think Charlie liked it, did you, Charlie?'

'Why not?' protested Charlie.

'You didn't look as if you was enjoying it. Too much blood,' Bet whispered confidentially to Moggy. 'I think he's got a weak stomach.'

Suddenly Moggy felt a tap on his shoulder. Turning round he saw Clara and Vicky standing in the gangway.

'Hallo,' said Vicky.

A new bout was just starting and the people around began to hiss to them to be quiet, so Moggy beckoned the two girls to sit down alongside them and the five of them watched the whole of the next fight through in silence. When it was finished Vicky leant across and spoke to Moggy.

'How do you feel?'

'What do you mean?'

'You took quite a hammering.'

'Oh!' said Moggy. 'It don't hurt when you've won. What did you come for?'

'To watch you fight, fat-head, why do you think? It were all right.'

Moggy sat silently for a moment. 'Where's Jan?' he asked as casually as he could manage. 'He said he might come.'

'He's around,' replied Vicky non-committally.

'Do you still go with him?'

Vicky nodded and looked away. 'Sometimes.'

'Give him my love,' said Moggy bitterly.

'What's up with Jan?' asked Bet.

'The bastard planted a meat-hook on me. I felt his hand on my coat but I never thought.'

'He had to get rid of it,' said Vicky. 'He explained.'

'Tell me why,' said Moggy. 'I've been dying to know.'

'It's the army. They wouldn't take him if he was caught with it.'

'That's true,' put in Clara. 'It didn't matter so much to you.'

'What's it got to do with you?' snapped Moggy.

'Sorry I spoke,' she replied primly.

'Clara's got another boy friend,' jeered Bet. 'I've seen them out.'

'I'll break my heart,' said Moggy sarcastically.

Charlie grabbed his brother by the arm. 'What're you going to do to Jan?' he asked. 'You never did finish that fight.'

'Which fight?'

'The one at school, remember?'

'You'll have to hurry if you want to find him,' said Vicky. 'He's leaving next week. To join up.'

'That was quick, weren't it? He didn't say nothing when I saw him.'

'He heard a couple of days ago. He's going as a boy soldier.'

'Ready for the next war,' commented Moggy. 'He reckons he knows all about it already.'

'Are you going to fight him?' urged Charlie.

'Chuck it, will you, kid?' said Moggy wearily. 'It don't make no difference now. Tell you what! You fight him for me.'

'Is the kid going to be a puggy too?' asked Vicky.

'He'll be better than me.'

'Don't be daft,' protested Bet.

'Oh, yes, he will. Ask Bob Tranter.'

They settled back to watch the boxing again. At the end of the bout Vicky and Clara announced that they were not going to stay any longer. As Vicky walked up the gangway, Clara hung back.

'See you, Mog,' she said at last. She waited for a moment as if hoping that Moggy would break the ice.

He was about to suggest that they might meet up that evening when he caught sight of Bet's mocking eyes. 'See you, Clara,' he mumbled. 'See you around.'

Clara smiled briefly at him before turning to follow Vicky.

'Are you staying long?' Bet asked Moggy.

'Charlie and I want to see the big one, don't we, kid?' replied Moggy. Bet moved around restlessly in her seat, until Moggy nudged her irritably. 'Beat it if you want to. But if you're going to stay, just sit still.'

Bet sank deeper in her chair and pouted, but her sulks did not last long, and she stayed to watch the remaining bouts with her brothers.

It was after six o'clock before Moggy led Charlie and Bet out of the crowded hall. The sweat of competitors and audience and the heavy tobacco smoke combined with the heat of late August to make the atmosphere almost intolerable. Outside, however, a fresh wind had risen, which whipped up the dust from the dry streets. People seemed to be just emerging from their houses to find their entertainment for the evening. From a neighbouring street came the endlessly repetitive sound of a barrel organ.

'When're you going to get a fight, Charlie?' asked Moggy.

'I hadn't thought,' replied his brother.

'It's about time you started thinking, ain't it? It's all right learning with Bob, but you've got to fight some time. Otherwise you don't get no proper opposition.'

'You're the pug, Moggy,' exclaimed Charlie uncertainly. 'I ain't like you.'

'Christ, kid, you're great,' exclaimed Moggy. 'Better than me.'

'Who gave you that line?'

'Bob Tranter, of course. He reckons he's got a future champion in you.'

'I thought you was going to be the champion, Mog,' put in Bet.

Moggy grabbed his sister round the waist. 'Like you was going to get hitched to a swell.'

'I still might at that,' she said primly as she disentangled herself from his grasp.

'You've made your mind up,' said Moggy.

'Like you've made up your mind to be a boxer,' replied his sister. 'I reckon you'd knock spots off Charlie any time, Mog.'

'Go on; he's got the style.' Moggy made a few passes at a lamp post in as classic a style as he could muster. 'I'm just brute force and ignorance.'

'Yes, but you wants to win,' insisted Bet. 'You wants to win worse than anything. And you've got a mean streak. Ain't that right, Charlie?'

Charlie seemed to be embarrassed by the turn in the conversation. 'I don't know,' he mumbled.

'You ain't lost a fight yet.'

Moggy quickly corrected her. 'I have.'

'That one don't count,' she protested.

'They all count. Anyway, you can't compare me with Charlie. He ain't started properly yet.'

'He won't neither. Want to bet? Takes life too easy. Besides, I told you, it turns him up.'

Moggy looked to Charlie to defend himself, but his brother was trailing his feet in the gutter, pretending not to listen.

'It's up to Charlie, ain't it?' said Moggy impatiently. 'Nobody's forcing him to do nothing.'

'Charlie's like our dad,' said his sister. 'Ain't got no ideas. Bet he'll be a dockie too.'

'What's so wrong with that?' demanded Charlie. 'Moggy's a dockie too.'

'Not now I ain't.'

'What do you mean?' asked Charlie, surprised.

'They've blacked me.' The two of them looked blankly at him so he spelt it out. 'They won't give me no work.'

Bet looked at him for a moment and then gave a squeal of laughter. 'What have you done, then, Mog?'

'Had a bit of a punch up with the rozzers.'

'You never!' declared Bet.

'Is that what you was on about, back in there?' asked Charlie. 'The hook Jan planted on you.'

'Yeh,' said Moggy. 'I don't know it mattered, though. They'd probably have done me anyway.' He grinned and thrashed out at the air. 'I didn't half have a go at the law.'

'Does Dad know?' asked Bet.

'No. I ain't told him yet.'

'What's he going to say?' she asked in hushed tones.

'Look!' said Moggy firmly. 'It don't matter, do it? I decide what I'm going to do, not him.'

'You're going to be a puggy,' chanted Bet. 'World champion.'

'You'll need a job meantime,' put in Charlie.

Bet was not to be put off by such mundane considerations. 'You'll be the puggy. I'll – ' Bet paused and examined her reflection in a shop window. 'Do you think he'll have me?' she asked.

'Who?' asked Moggy.

'My swell, of course.'

'Only if he's deaf, dumb, blind and stupid,' retorted Charlie.

Bet punched Charlie on the arm. 'I didn't ask your opinion.' She shoved her face close to Moggy's. 'What do you think, Mog?'

'He's as good as a goner,' he pronounced.

Bet looked across at Charlie, as if he were a lower form of life. 'And he's only going to be a dockie.'

'Tell you what, Charlie,' said Moggy, half seriously, 'you be a dockie and work for the union. Don't pay no attention to what Dad says. You could get into Parliament if you played your cards right.'

'Him in Parliament?' jeered Bet. 'Can you see him?'

'Shut your gob, will you, Bet?' There was real anger in Charlie's voice. He had been taunted enough.

'He's as much chance of getting into Parliament as I have of being world champion,' declared Moggy.

Moggy was not banking on being world, or even

national, champion. All he wanted was to earn enough to set himself up in business in a small way. He could just see himself with a little pub or a newspaper shop – and not in Wapping if he could help it.

'Course you're going to be a champion,' protested Bet. 'How much did you win today?'

'Two quid.'

'Two bloody quid. Cor! Let's see the rhino, Mog.'

Moggy thrust his hand into his pocket as if to protect the money, but he let her pull it out and open his fingers one by one. Two pound notes lay crumpled on the palm of his hand.

'Cor,' cooed Bet again. 'Two of them.'

'I makes them, didn't you know?' said Moggy.

'What're you going to do with them, Mog?' asked Charlie.

Moggy lifted one of the notes and slipped it back into his pocket. 'Reckon I owes Bob Tranter that one.' He held up the second in front of his eyes, between the forefinger and thumb of both hands. 'Beautiful, ain't it?' He looked from his brother to his sister. 'Tell you what,' he said. 'Toss you for it.' He crumpled the note into his left fist and produced a penny from his right pocket. 'Heads or tails.'

'Tails,' shouted Bet as the coin spun into the air.

Moggy caught it on the palm of his right hand and turned it on to the back of his left.

'Heads,' he announced.

With a swift movement he returned both the pound and the penny to his pocket. Bet pounced on him with a cry of rage.

'I didn't see,' she protested.

'Course you didn't,' retorted Moggy. 'I ain't that stupid.'

She made a despairing attempt to force her way into his pocket, but he pushed her away with a laugh.

'That ain't fair,' she protested.

'Nothing's fair in this life, kid,' said Moggy. 'It's about time you learnt.'

Moggy pulled his sister to him and ran his fingers

through her tangled hair. 'Tell you what, kid, I'll give you a tanner.'

'And Charlie?' she asked.

'On his side now, are you? All right, if you say so. Tanner for you and a tanner for Charlie.'

'That leaves nineteen bob for you,' she grumbled.

'Look! I won it. And remember I'm out of work. It's all there is between me and the workhouse.'

'Ah,' said Bet soothingly. 'Poor Mog. We'll look after him, won't we, Charlie?'

Charlie stopped dragging his feet in the gutter and looked across at his brother. 'He don't need looking after.'

A new thought suddenly flashed across Bet's brain. 'Here, do you know what Liz told me?' she asked.

'What?' asked Moggy.

'When they went to shut up the Garden last night one of the day-time sleepers wouldn't move. It was Lushy Sue.'

'Cor,' said Charlie. 'She must have missed opening time. First time in history.'

'She were dead,' announced Bet. 'Stiff as a board and all cold!'

'You lot must have plagued the life out of her.'

Bet ignored Moggy's accusation. 'I was thinking back there when I was bored. You know the way rats leave a sinking ship?'

'That's what they say,' agreed Moggy.

'They do, really,' insisted Bet. 'Do you reckon the lice climbs out of Lushy Sue's hair, or do they get buried with her?'

'Don't be daft,' said Moggy with a laugh. 'It don't matter one way or the other.'

'It do if you're a lice.'

'Louse,' corrected Charlie.

'What do you mean?' Bet asked, puzzled.

'Louse is singular. Lice is plural.'

Bet nudged Moggy. 'I reckon our Charlie'll be a teacher. He spouts like one.' She returned to her main line of argument. 'It do matter if you're a louse. It can't be much fun being shut up in a grave six foot underground, with Lushy Sue all rotting. She ponged bad enough when she was alive.'

'You reckon the rats have got the right idea, do you?' asked Moggy.

'Too blooming right, they have,' replied Bet. 'You know what I reckon? If there's just one thing worth knowing in life, it's when to get off the bleeding ship.'

The Outsiders

S. E. HINTON

'You know what a greaser is?' Bob asked. 'White trash with long hair.'

I felt the blood draining from my face. 'You know what a Soc is? White trash with Mustangs and madras.' And then, because I couldn't think of anything bad enough to call them, I spat at them.

Bob shook his head, smiling slowly. 'You could use a bath, greaser. And a good working over.'

The Soc caught my arm and twisted it behind my back, and shoved my face into the fountain. I fought, but the hand at the back of my neck was strong. I'm drowning, I thought, they've gone too far . . .

The Outsiders is an authentic and moving book written by a teenager about teenagers. It was published originally in America where it has already sold over 1,500,000 copies in paperback.

That Was Then This Is Now and *Rumble Fish* by S. E. Hinton are also in LIONS.

I NEVER LOVED YOUR MIND

Paul Zindel

'Look, Dewey-Smewey whateverthehellyournameis. Don't put me in the same class with you. You come off like a lazy spoiled punk whose Momsy and Popsy think they're committing some type of middle-class progressiveness by letting you drop out of school because you belly-ached too much. I think you're just one more of our sick society's ridiculous, dangerous wastes. That's what I think.'

So Yvette, idealist, vegetarian, burdened by her concern for society's evils, takes a verbal swipe at Dewey, clever, curious and friendly. But he catches her out, and gradually they realise that perhaps they do have something in common.

'Highly topical, this is a crazily funny and crazily moving love (or non-love) story between a boy and girl around 17 or 18, in the Holden Caulfield line. Clever stuff.'

The Observer

The Pigman, My Darling, My Hamburger, and *Pardon Me, You're Stepping on My Eyeball!* are also in Fontana Lions.